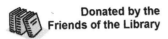

# Instructions
# for the
# End of the
# World

ALSO BY JAMIE KAIN

*The Good Sister*

# Instructions
# for the
# End of the
# World

JAMIE KAIN

St. Martin's Griffin

New York

INSTRUCTIONS FOR THE END OF THE WORLD. Copyright © 2015 by Jamie Kain. All rights reserved. Printed in the United States of America. For information, address St. Martin's Press, 175 Fifth Avenue, New York, N.Y. 10010.

www.stmartins.com

The Library of Congress Cataloging-in-Publication Data is available upon request.

ISBN 978-1-250-04786-1 (hardcover)
ISBN 978-1-250-04785-4 (e-book)

Our books may be purchased in bulk for promotional, educational, or business use. Please contact your local bookseller or the Macmillan Corporate and Premium Sales Department at (800) 221-7945, extension 5442, or by e-mail at Macmillan SpecialMarkets@macmillan.com.

First Edition: December 2015

10　9　8　7　6　5　4　3　2　1

*To Genevieve*

# Instructions for the End of the World

# PART ONE

# The End of the World
# as We Know It

*August 3, 2002*

By the time you return, maybe the end will have come.

The End, as in the apocalypse, or the next ice age, or the Second Coming, or whatever.

Your leaving feels like the end of something, but I don't know what.

Maybe you think I never really listened closely enough, never took your warnings seriously, but I did. I remember everything.

You said the world might end in fire, or in ice, and that the how of it didn't matter so much as the importance of being prepared for the worst.

You said only the strongest would survive.

You said we would need a careful plan, and a foolproof backup plan.

You prepared us for every possible disaster scenario— except this one.

So what do we do when the apocalypse happens from the inside? When it's our family, and not civilization itself, that falls apart?

While you were busy preparing for catastrophe, maybe the worst really did happen, and it wasn't what you thought it would be at all.

# One

WOLF

*July 6, 2002*

From the edge of the forest, you can catch the world unaware. You can watch like a silent animal, and you can observe what people don't want you to see.

If you were the one sitting in the crook of the madrone tree, you would hear the car and the truck on the gravel road before you saw them emerge into the clearing and stop in front of a forlorn house.

A man gets out of the white truck and walks to the driver's side of the car, where a woman sits inside without opening the door. He tries the door handle, but it must be locked. Then he says something. It looks as if they are having a standoff.

Their vehicles are new, shiny, clean, waxed, like cars in commercials—a silver sedan and the large white truck, which is towing a matching white camper trailer. These are nothing like the dusty cars in which I have grown up riding.

Adjusting myself in the crook of the tree to keep my left leg from falling asleep, I press my shoulder into the chill of the wood. The madrone is called the refrigerator tree because even on the hottest days it feels cold to the touch. No one really knows why. I am grateful for it on this day when the heat bears down like a malevolent force.

I sit still and silent, practicing this skill. It's what I imagine the Native Americans did in these woods hundreds of years ago, before white people came.

After awhile I am rewarded with the sight of a hare, its dust-brown fur stretched over a long, lean body, as it eases out of a burrow. A few seconds later the ears of several baby hares poke up, their velvet black eyes peering out at the world, looking for their mother. I know from watching that they won't venture out, not until she invites them to do so in whatever silent language of movement they use. She will nudge them back into the burrow again and again, until they are large enough to search out food and fast enough to evade predators.

And even then, only a few of them will survive, if they're lucky.

I understand the balance nature seeks—the need for the hawk to eat the hare—but I have never felt at peace with its harshness. I don't begin to understand why life, so excruciatingly fragile, so breathtaking in its delicate beauty, can be destroyed with such ease. Mahesh would say that no life is truly destroyed, that it just returns to the Great Mother Earth to live again, but tell that to the hare trying to keep her babies alive.

Then again, she probably understands it far better than I do.

Finally the woman, small and dark-haired, gets out of the car and stands next to it, arms crossed over her chest, posture stiff as a redwood. Then she picks her way across the overgrown yard and up onto the porch, followed by the man.

If you were the one watching now, you would know the rush of pleasure to see the girl who climbs out of the passenger seat of the pickup truck and follows after her parents. Although I am too far away for fine details, I get the general impression of her: long dark hair in a braid down her back, narrow limbs, jeans, a white tank top. A species unto herself, she moves without seeming the least bit disturbed by her unkempt surroundings.

Last to exit, from the car, is another girl. She looks like her sister, but smaller and I assume younger. The colors she wears are jarring in this dusty place—bright pink and turquoise. She calls out something to the others, then does a ridiculous skitter across the yard, like a Jesus lizard on water.

I watch, and I gather facts: a new family in the valley, neighbors where, for almost as long as I can remember, there have been none, save the angry old man who used to live in the house only a handful of times each year, using it as a place to stay while he hunted deer. Already I feel encroached upon, hemmed in. I am one whose territory has just been shrunk by development.

It's a feeling that's been gnawing at me even before this new arrival. It started with my mother coming back a month ago.

You might wonder why I watch, and that, you would be wise to question. It's the big why.

Of the facts I might choose to tell about myself, I can think of none worth knowing. I sit here in the woods because it is a halfway point between the place others choose to call my home and the place I choose to call my home. I am often hovering in between, unclear about my destination.

The first home has gotten too crowded for me, with the return of my mother, Annika Dietrich.

She of the little white pills, the empty wine bottles, the bottomless need.

When she left last year, it was a relief, like having a painful tooth removed, followed by the shock of realizing that there is a hole where the tooth once lived. And then, as with all things, you change. You adapt. A year passes, or more than a year. You stop missing the tooth, you learn to chew on the other side of your mouth, and when you remember it, you recall only the pain it caused and your relief at its removal.

But my mother is not a molar, or even a canine tooth. She is an addict. A recovering one, she says, but I'm seventeen years old. What am I going to do with a full-blown mother now? What do I do with her new twelve-step religion, her higher power, or her pseudo Jesus talk that fits in at the village about as well as a snake in a henhouse?

I have no use for it, so I disappear into the trees, which are the only caretakers I've known who never disappoint.

Okay, I don't completely disappear.

I am building a shelter. A secret tree house, tiny in size but big on promise.

I will soon be living like my hero, Thoreau, with his cabin in the woods. Only higher.

And maybe when it's finished I will build a bridge to the moon.

I will learn what the crystalline perfection of solitude has to teach me.

The family has gone inside the house, leaving behind a silence that fills the clearing. Even the cicadas are quiet for a stretch of time. I'm about to climb down from the tree to look for a place less encroached upon when I hear the front screen door squeak open and slap shut again. I look up to see the man and the older girl there, the one not intimidated by weeds. He says something and hands the girl a rifle.

A gun?

It is long, black, ominous in the sunlight.

In a fluid motion, she rests the weight of the rifle against her shoulder as if she's handled it a thousand times, and I watch, dumbstruck, as she heads toward the woods—and toward me.


NICOLE

Everything is a test.

If I flinch, I fail.

If I say no, I fail.

If I hesitate, I fail.

I have learned how to survive being my father's daughter, even if that's not what he thinks he's been preparing me for.

So I march across the field toward the woods, Daddy's good little soldier girl.

All you need to know about Lieutenant Colonel (Retired) James Reed you can learn by reading his self-published book, *The End of the World As We Know It*, a manual on surviving the apocalypse, or the next ice age, or the mega-earthquake, or whatever catastrophe finally befalls mankind.

For his money, he's betting on social and government collapse caused by widespread shortages of food and water brought on by natural disaster. It's as good a theory as any, I guess.

What I always wonder, but never ask aloud, is: if there's a God, what makes us think he even wants us to survive?

I know what my dad's answer would be. He'd say we are God's chosen, created in his image and given the knowledge and talent to survive any catastrophes we face.

But what if my dad's book falls into the hands of someone who isn't chosen? This is what I would then ask, if I were a different person, in a different life, far, far from here. My idea of God is different from his.

My dad's book doesn't contain any chapters about himself personally. It is strictly a guide to how to skin game animals, purify water, find and build shelters, start a fire in any weather under any circumstances, set a broken bone with any materials on hand, and other such matters. Yet you can infer through the topics and his handling of them what kind of man would write a book like his.

You can make an educated guess.

And you'd be right.

James Reed is the kind of guy who brings his family to a new home none of us has ever seen before, aside from an old family photo, which he has decided we will live in, without seeking our opinions. So here we are, in the middle of nowhere. We all—myself, my mom, my sister Izzy—are varying levels of stunned and appalled.

Me: approximately 40 percent stunned, 15 percent appalled, 45 percent I-don't-know-what. Intrigued, maybe?

Mom: 60 percent stunned, 40 percent appalled.

Izzy: 30 percent stunned, 60 percent appalled, 10 percent worried about her hair.

The place Dad has brought us is not like anywhere we have lived before, and we've lived in a lot of places, thanks to my dad's army career. It's the home my great-great-grandparents built over a hundred and fifty years ago with money they made selling groceries to miners during the Gold Rush. It's a crumbling two-story Victorian, oddly out of place in this rugged landscape, hunched quietly here in a clearing like an old lady waiting to die, with the forest standing vigil around her. I guess the color of the house used to be white, though most of the paint has peeled off to reveal the grayish siding beneath.

There are woods on all sides, in a landscape of rolling hills that get higher to the west, as foothills turn into steep mountains. And even though this is a family home, I've never been here before because my dad wasn't close to my grandparents, or his grandparents, and no one has lived here full time since I don't know when. He's the only child, so he inherited the house last year when my grandfather died.

I tried to picture the place before we got here, but it's so remote that I could barely find the area on a map.

And Dad isn't exactly interested in the same details the rest of the world is. He told us only that it had a cellar for canned goods and a big detached garage added in the sixties, where Dad would keep all his interminable supplies that he stocks away like a crazed squirrel preparing for the world's longest winter. He said it was twenty acres in the Sierra foothills, mostly wooded but with a good clear area for a two-acre garden and some livestock, with its own underground well, a year-round stream, and a septic system.

So there is what I pictured, with my sad lack of useful information, and there is reality.

Our home for the foreseeable future is the most broken-down house I have ever seen outside of a horror movie. I can only hope the plumbing works, which occurs to me because Dad is big on lecturing us about living without plumbing—how we take running water and flushing toilets for granted, how we'd all be better off using an outhouse because it would toughen us up.

Mom will not, even for a night, use an outhouse.

She was born in Cambodia in the seventies, her earliest memories of starvation and hiding in the jungle. Once, in a rare moment of willingness to talk about herself, she told me how she saw her older brother shot in the back as they were escaping the massacre of her village by the Khmer Rouge. When she was six years old her parents were able to immigrate with her and her remaining siblings to the US, to Southern California, where they went on to have what must have felt like a shockingly normal suburban life when contrasted with what came before.

So it kind of makes sense to me that she will not consider accepting anything but middle-class living conditions. Even with Dad's plans to renovate this house to its former glory, it doesn't come anywhere near meeting her standards.

I think of our pristine ranch house in the desert, and I don't miss it, but I know my mother does. Our neighborhood always seemed to me like a place without a soul, like where zombies would choose to live if they had jobs and bank accounts. Yet I think Mom sees the suburbs as the kind of place murderous dictators never take over and slaughter millions of people. She kept our house spotlessly clean and free of clutter. And she is a fan of all things new and improved—two categories this house does not fall into.

Our arrival at our new home was preceded by ten hours of driving through the desert and the Central Valley. We left at oh four hundred hours, which means early morning, before daylight, in case you don't know military time speak. Mom drove her Honda with Izzy in the passenger seat, and I rode with Dad in his truck, which was towing the camper trailer full of the last of our household stuff. A moving company will be delivering the rest of it.

We got a five-minute tour of the house, during which I was relieved to see it does have an old, funky bathroom, along with a bedroom for each of us. There is even a decrepit sort of charm about the place, if you consider haunted houses charming. Then we were given our jobs—Izzy and Dad unloading the trailer, me finding dinner, Mom standing in the kitchen looking appalled.

She is so angry I'm not even sure she knows the words to express her rage. This is not a good sign, but Dad is a pro at ignoring female emotions. He's been doing it for years.

Finding dinner, to most people, might mean opening up the refrigerator or picking up a take-out menu. Not in my family. In the Reed household, we find dinner the old-fashioned way whenever possible. Or at least my dad and I do.

My mother and little sister have not signed on for this particular survivalist lifestyle. They have not learned to assimilate.

For my mother, survival mode isn't a lifestyle choice. It's what her family came to America to escape. And they did escape. From age six onward she grew up in Long Beach and learned to love all things American and middle class. She has no romantic notions about roughing it—which these days for her means skipping a weekly pedicure.

So I am the girl with the hunting rifle, forever traipsing into the woods hoping to take down something more impressive (and better tasting) than a squirrel. But this is not the right time of day for hunting, in the glaring heat of the late afternoon. This is when animals lie low, waiting for the heat to pass. After the sun dips below the ridgeline, there will surely be deer, rabbit, and other game, though early in the morning is best, when animals are first venturing out to find food for the day.

But Dad likes to make things hard for me. He wants to know I will survive no matter what happens. Without the son he always hoped for, he's forced to pass on his knowledge to me, since Izzy mostly refuses to participate in anything remotely outdoorsy.

I, on the other hand, am happiest surrounded by trees and sky.

Picking my way along a trail mostly overgrown with brush, I feel the cool metal weight of the barrel and stock in my hands. There are two emotions I waver between. One is reluctance to fire a gun, killing some poor animal that's just trying to live its life. In my head, I don't comply with every order just to please my dad.

In real life, though, I am my father's daughter, and the other feeling is pride. I am really good at hunting. I can shoot a duck out of the air with one quick shot, then clean the carcass and fry it up for dinner over an open fire, if I have to. As much as I sometimes get tired of my dad's constant prepping, I do like knowing I can take care of myself. I've never liked confronting the death of an animal, but I understand that it's how we get food to eat.

"Let's go find dinner," he will say at the start of every hunting trip, and I go.

There is always that moment when I contemplate my options, consider saying no. Maybe declare myself vegetarian, just to see his reaction. But I never do. I am only a rebel in my mind.

The heat sears my skin and sends rivulets of sweat trickling down my back and my rib cage. My tank top sticks to me and I wish I had something cooler than jeans and boots on, though I know stinging nettle is all around and they are protecting me from the pain of that horrible weed, at least.

In the woods, my senses sharpen. Here on the edge of field and woods is my best chance to find game. I choose a tree trunk to lean against and grow still and quiet, slow my breathing, and wait. Gnats fly at my face, but I don't swat them away.

Soon enough, I get lucky and hear a rustling near a fallen tree. Easing closer, I see a lean brown hare, and I lift the rifle.

I have the hare in my sight when I hear a voice yell, "Stop!"

Startled, I nearly fire the gun, but my father's training kicks in. I force my fingers to ease off the trigger, lower the gun halfway as the hare disappears into the brush, and turn toward the sound of the voice.

A guy my age, wavy brown, too-long hair, is descending a tree. The way he's dressed—all faded brown and green—I might never have spotted him if he hadn't spoken up.

"That hare has babies," he calls as he reaches the ground.

He looks at the rifle and hesitates, so I lower it all the way.

"That was my dinner," I say under my breath, but with no feeling.

He comes closer and I tense, wondering who he is and why he's here on our property.

In a tree.

Watching me, apparently.

But as he nears, I see there is something about him that's wide open, honest, not the least bit threatening. He has gold-brown eyes that glow like his skin, as if he's somehow lit from within, a lantern shaped like a teenage boy. He is almost pretty, but with features that are a little too hard to be feminine. I watch him, my mouth dry and dumb, until he stops a few feet away and holds out his hand a little awkwardly, as if he's never done it before.

"I'm Wolf," he says.

I look down at the extended hand, the incongruity of it, as if we are conducting a business deal in the woods. He does not look like the kind of guy who worries about formalities. When I don't extend my hand to his, he turns his palm up and smiles.

"I bear no weapons," he says. "Isn't that what the handshake was originally meant to communicate?"

I lower the gun until it points straight at the ground. "I'm hunting," I reply.

Stupidly.

What kind of sixteen-year-old girl hunts for her dinner? is the question that forms in my head when I see myself through this Wolf's eyes. I normally don't worry much about such things, since I am strictly forbidden from dating or even contemplating the existence of boys (and what does it say about me, that I am willing to comply with such rules?), but this guy is like no one I've ever seen before.

"Right," he says, one eyebrow arching as if this is some kind of joke I don't get. "What's your name?"

"Nicole. What were you doing in our tree?" I say.

"Nice to meet you, Nicole." He looks up at the tree then, as if the answer to my question might be found in its branches. "I didn't realize it was your tree."

My face burns and I have no idea what to say. I have accidentally become a bizarre caricature of a hick, standing here with my gun, bickering over property lines.

"You didn't answer my question."

"I was just enjoying the quiet. It gets kind of crowded where I live sometimes."

"Which is where?"

"Sadhana Village," he says, his head tilting east. "You know it?"

I guess my blank look answers for me, because when I say nothing, he goes on. "It's adjacent to your property—a spiritual retreat center."

"You mean that yoga place? We passed a sign for it. I didn't realize people live there."

"Yeah, it's a self-sufficient village. There are about a hundred of us that live there full time."

I blink at this, recalling my father's comments about the sign when we passed it on the road. He muttered about hippies and told me to stay the hell away from "those people."

From this guy.

"Oh," I say, as understanding dawns that I'm talking to a hippie. A real live one, not a character from a movie or a person in a Woodstock photo in my history textbook.

My stomach does a stupid little flip-flop and I feel, suddenly, like the uncoolest girl on the planet.

I become conscious, in an awkwardly sweaty way, that I'm alone with this disheveled guy in the middle of the woods. I've been around guys—normal guys who wear logo T-shirts and jeans and talk about football—but I've never been alone with one. Not really alone.

This guy Wolf has a gaze that makes me feel like he sees into my soul or something. He stares straight into my eyes without blinking, and there is an unnerving stillness about him. I've never been looked at quite like this.

I blink first, look down at the ground, then look back up to find him still staring. It's like no one has ever told him staring is rude.

"I have to go," I say.

He nods, and his gaze finally drops to the rifle. "Right, your dinner."

I don't say bye. I just head in the direction the hare ran. I won't find it, I know. I wouldn't have the heart to shoot it now even if I did.

Sometimes I think there is no uglier power than the kind that exists when I have a loaded gun in my hands—the power to destroy, with the pull of a trigger, all the complicated and miraculous work of creation.

It's the way of the world, my father would say, and our job is to come out on top in the game of survival.

But what if he's wrong?

What if he's wrong about everything?

It's the question that nags at me more and more these days.

# Two

---

ISABEL

I am not going to live in this haunted old roach motel. I am not, I am not, I am *not*.

My dad is the king of Crazyland.

He wears a Crazy hat and talks his Crazy talk, and for as long as I can remember, my dumb sister has believed him. I saw how crazy he was before I was even old enough to ride a bike, but Nic? She's brainwashed.

I remember him talking about how we're going to run out of food and water, back when I was a little kid, and I was like, Duh. We can just go to the store and buy more. Have you even seen Safeway? It's got enough food in it to last us forever. I was even sure that was the problem—that he'd never been inside a grocery store, because Mom does all the food shopping and cooking, or at least she used to.

So as I am glaring at the disgusting old craphole that Dad claims is going to be my new bedroom, I know he's gone from his old kind of crazy to a whole new level, complete with delusions that involve me. It started sometime soon after 9/11. When the whole world was freaking out, my dad was having a total mental break. This house, and this bedroom, are the final straw for me.

First off?

There is this dark brown wood paneling and the green shaggy carpet that smells like a dog's been smoking a pack a day in here, and I'm like, seriously?

No, really.

Seriously?

I can't say a word, because if I talk back I'll get an hour-long lecture and some horrible list of chores that will involve chopping wood and scrubbing the mangy toilet with a tooth-brush. So I pop my gum, as my sole protest to this retarded situation.

I mean, seriously.

My hair is getting all puffy and weird from the heat in here, the land of no air-conditioning, and I want to find the nearest mirror to try to save it from oblivion, but I have already caught a glimpse of the bathroom, which I will not ever, ever, ever be using. It's got a green tub, a green sink, and . . . are you ready for this?

A green toilet.

And not just any shade of green.

I heard my mom muttering something about ugly avocado, but it's like totally the color of a swamp, the color of things dying, the color green crayon you would choose if you wanted to draw an ogre or show someone the color of ugly.

It's Shrek green.

Dad has moved on to showing Nic her room, so I slip back down the stairs to the main hallway and out onto the decrepit back porch, where I dig my compact out of my purse and set it on the railing so I can see my reflection as I start braiding my hair. At least if it's in two tight braids the puffiness will have no chance of increasing. Then I notice that all my lip gloss is gone.

I am ridiculously, strictly forbidden by Dad from wearing makeup, but I have somewhat successfully argued that lip gloss doesn't count as makeup because it's clear (well, sort of) and it's purely for keeping my lips from getting dry and cracked (okay, not at all). Dad didn't really okay the lip gloss wearing, but he mostly doesn't notice when I do wear it. He also forbids us from all the normal things girls are supposed to do to better themselves, like getting our ears or anything else pierced, getting highlights, wearing cute clothes, or wearing shoes with any kind of heel.

If my dad had his way, I'd be wearing a neck-to-floor pioneer girl dress, with my hair all sad and plain and grown down to my knees (with a bunch of split ends, for sure, because Dad doesn't believe in spending money on unnecessary things like girl haircuts), and some kind of granny boots that lace up to, like, my armpits or something—better for keeping the boys away.

He seriously thinks that's how girls our age are supposed to dress.

Seriously.

His head would explode if he found the stash of makeup I keep hidden in the bottom of my purse, or the outfits I've saved my own money to buy—that I hardly ever get to wear—with Mom's help. Mom doesn't agree with Dad about the clothes and makeup stuff, but she says she has to choose her battles, whatever that means. I think it mostly means she goes along with whatever he says, and then when he's not looking she does what she wants.

So I figure it's all right with her if I do the same thing.

I am just finishing up my second braid when I hear Mom's voice rise from its normal tone into an angry shriek, and I bite my lip, wondering where I can go to escape the argument.

That's always my first instinct, but then I realize she's yelling about this house and how she refuses to live in it, and this could be an important argument to be present for. I might be able to support the cause of us getting the hell out of here.

Probably not, I decide on second thought, but I have to hear what Dad says, so I ease my way back inside just in time to witness something I've never seen before in all my parents' years of fighting.

Right after my dad says, "Shut up for a minute, Maly," my mom slaps him across the face.

It's not the first time he's ever told her to shut up, but it's the first time she's ever hit him, far as I know. My eyes have gone wide, but I hurry to rearrange my face in a way that says all this is no big deal, that I haven't even noticed what's happening, because if Dad sees me gawking, there's no telling what punishment he might concoct later. Skinning a chicken, digging rocks out of the garden . . .

For a long moment, it feels like everything stands still. My father is in shock that my mother has slapped him, and he stands there blinking, his face turning pink with anger, the reddish outline of my mom's small handprint deepening on his cheek.

I think the heat must be making her crazy like him.

I catch a movement across the room and realize it's Nic standing there, witnessing the scene too.

Her dumb face is pale, her mouth slack.

That my mom has not only dared to hit my dad, but that she's done it in front of us kids—it's a situation so freakish that it feels as if the air between us all is crackling with an electrical current.

And then the current is broken when my father lifts his hand as if to grab my mother's arm, but she screeches, "Don't you touch me!" and dodges his grasp.

A moment later, she has run from the house, and my dad follows after. Nicole follows them both, probably thinking she's going to jump in and save the situation like a good daughter, but I only want to watch and see who the winner will be. I am of course cheering silently for Mom, but for my whole life she's not exactly been a worthy opponent for our brick wall of a father.

Outside, I am surprised to see not more fighting but my dad catching my mom in his grasp and hugging her to him as she struggles and cries. After a little bit of fighting she goes limp in his arms, and my hope of Mom getting us out of this house vanishes before my eyes.


## NICOLE

My parents don't fight like this, at least not in front of us girls.

Fighting takes two participants, and my dad, as a rule,

does not participate. There are times like now, when my mom gets mad. She will start trying to tell him something, and when he doesn't respond she starts complaining in a heavier and heavier Khmer accent until she is speaking no English at all, and then when he still doesn't respond she will go storming around the house slamming doors and objects as she cleans.

This is a scene I've witnessed countless times growing up, and when I was little I thought it was my mom who was acting badly. As I've grown older, though, I have had to rethink that idea.

Which is harder to do than it sounds.

What if one person is mad and the other person ignores it, over and over again? What if the person you are supposed to care most about in the world has a problem and you refuse to do anything about it? What if you pretend they're not talking to you at all?

It is past midnight. I am lying in a sleeping bag in the dark, curled up on my side, a pillow hugged against my chest.

Mom's ranting, Dad's silence.

He has a way of being silent that is louder than any voice.

"You never asked me," she is saying. "You just take us here and you don't ask me what I want."

I can sort of understand why he tunes out. My mother's message is always the same, or nearly the same. She has a standard list of complaints that goes something like: you didn't ask me what I want, you don't listen, you don't care.

Extra things get thrown in, depending on the situation that's upset her. Like now: this house is a dump, it's in the middle of nowhere, there are wild animals outside, bugs everywhere, no people around, you are acting crazy.

This last accusation hits me in the gut, causes me to hug my pillow closer, as if the insult was leveled at me and not Dad.

I don't know why.

I do know why.

Because it's true, and I don't want it to be.

I don't know how we are supposed to recover from crazy. I don't know where we go from there.

My dad, mostly competent, mostly okay, seems to have come a little unhinged since retiring from the military. It's as if the structure of life in the army showed him how to act, what to believe, how to be, and then things started to unravel when we were all shown by a group of terrorists just how illusory our ideas of safety really are.

And now, free to make his own choices, he is leading us astray.

My mother, never much of a willing follower in the first place, is a problem he probably should have considered long ago.

She has been looking forward to his retirement as the time when she could finally go back to school and focus on moving up in her own career. Dad had the idea that when we moved here to the middle of nowhere she would homeschool us, but Mom never seemed to be into that idea.

She has always been a regular teacher with her own second-grade classroom, and I know she loved having a whole room full of students. She most loved the difficult ones, and I remember from looking over her shoulder as she used the computer that she'd been checking out graduate programs in special education, learning disabilities, autism. She'd looked up the distance between our new home and the MIND Institute at UC Davis, which is apparently the new place to go for becoming an expert on autism. And later she'd filled out online grad school applications.

It wasn't hard to see that she would have considered teaching just me and Izzy, at home all day, about as interesting as watching grass grow, especially when there were kids out there who could have really used her help.

I'm not sure Dad ever truly heard her about any of her own goals or wishes. He definitely didn't understand, judging by the state of this house, that she has no intention of returning to the poverty she knew as a small child in Cambodia, if she can help it. She knows there are suburban stucco houses with pristine lawns, clean running water, master suites, luxury bathrooms, all within her reach if Dad would stop acting like the world is about to end next Thursday.

And why shouldn't she want that like everyone else?

My dad has been making me keep a notebook full of his survivalist wisdom for as long as I've been old enough to write complete sentences. I remember the very first entry I ever made, with him watching over me and telling me how to spell the words as we sat at the kitchen table after dinner one night. It went like this: "Survival means being able to rely on yourself, no matter what happens."

Back then, I was eight years old, and I didn't know what it meant even after Dad explained it. I had some ideas, like if I got lost in the woods, I'd have to find my own food and shelter, or if my parents were killed in a car wreck, I would have to live on my own or with a foster family. I sort of understood, but not really.

The part I didn't get, the part no amount of prepping can make clear, is that there is no one else who's going to save the day in the end. No one else is going to give you a hug and tell you everything will be okay.

## ISABEL

Today is the day my life stopped being my life.

Today is the day that will go down in history as the day when everything started to suck.

No, actually, *suck* is a completely inadequate word for what this day has done to my sense of the universe being a fair and nonretarded place.

The government should make it illegal for people like my dad to have kids.

This house only gets worse the longer we're in it. It's like if you were watching a horror movie, and in the movie the family pulled up to their new house with the moving van, you would scream in your head for them to back the fuck up and drive away, go live somewhere on the other side of the planet, because you know there's going to be some ghosts up in there, and people are going to die, and it's just not going to end well for anyone.

Consider my room.

I still am (considering it), and it's 1:14 a.m., according to the clock on my phone that no longer has a signal. I am lying wide awake, trying my best not to touch anything that I didn't pack and bring here from my old room. There is a brown stain on the ceiling above me, shaped like the edge of a continent, all uneven and weird. I stare at it, because I don't know what else to do.

I can't sleep.

I think about running away, but I don't have any friends or family for, like, a thousand miles, and I don't want to end up homeless. I mean, this is close enough to homeless, and I hate it, but at least there is running water, and food.

Apparently my great-grandmother died in this house, so it is probably haunted for real, but I haven't heard or seen any signs of ghosts yet.

*Yet.*

What I do hear is my mother's voice coming from below. She sounds like she is crying. She is yelling at my dad again, but he's not saying much back. The low rumble of his voice punctuates the rare moments when she is not yelling.

She has been freaking out ever since we pulled up in front of the house this afternoon. No, actually it started before that. She started getting really quiet during the drive, as we got further and further away from the nearest real city with restaurants and malls and big box stores.

My mom *loves* big box stores (so do I).

Then she started muttering in Khmer, always a bad sign.

My parents are in the room directly below me, so I can hear some of what she says now, mostly a broken record from earlier in the day, but she must be walking from room to room while she yells, because her voice comes and goes.

*Nasty old house . . . you never listen . . . don't care about any of us . . . not living in the middle of the woods . . .*

I hear enough bits and pieces to know that Mom has had it. Dad's finally pushed her over the edge with the move, and I am starting to feel hopeful again that she might actually win this battle, that Dad will realize we really can't live here, and he'll pack us up tomorrow and take us to a Marriott Suites until we can find a real house in a real city.

This is what *has* to happen, if the universe is even a little bit fair. This is what has to happen, if there is a God in heaven worth believing in. I'm not into praying or anything, but I close my eyes while I'm lying in my stupid red sleeping bag in my dusty old ceiling-stain room and I pray, "Dear God, Get us the fuck out of here, oh Lord. If you are listening, let us move somewhere decent tomorrow. Or right now, whichever is convenient for you. Amen."

I actually say that. Out loud.

And then I hear a door slam.

And then a car door.

And then the engine starting, and the car driving away. It all happens before I can get to the window and see who got into the car that's disappearing down the gravel road and into the woods now, but I pretty much know it's Mom.

I watch at the window until the taillights disappear, and then I go back to my sleeping bag, wipe my feet off with a towel because I don't want any old-house grime getting on my sleeping bag, and get back into it. The house is completely silent now. My mom is the queen of talking to herself when she's mad. She can have an hour-long argument with a wall, so I know by the silence it's definitely her who's left.

Where could she possibly go after one in the morning on a Tuesday night? No stores are open, no restaurants, nothing. Is she just going for a drive to cool off? Or is her leaving a bigger deal than that?

I picture her driving to a roadside chain motel and checking in, staying there for the night. But then what? Will she come back for us? Or at least for me?

How could she have left without me in the first place? I mean, okay, she was mad and she thought I was in bed asleep, so it doesn't make any sense that she'd come wake me up to take *me* to a motel with her.

I decide she must have just left to get away from this crappy house and my dad, to cool off and sleep somewhere clean for the night. This makes me feel a little better, but I still can't sleep. I look at my phone, at the stupid little No Service message on the screen, and I want to hurl it against the wall. Instead, I open up the text messages and stare at all the ones from my old friends—friends I might never see again.

I hate everything about my life. Everything.

I think about going downstairs and telling my dad that, right now. Telling him exactly how I feel. But I don't. Instead, I keep lying in my sleeping bag and staring at the stain on the ceiling, waiting wide-eyed for morning to come.

# Three

---

LAUREL

I can tell no one how happy I am that Annika has come home.

Who would understand?

Not Wolf, who sees his mother's presence as a noose around his neck.

Not Annika, who has never known what she really is to me.

Not my parents, who left fourteen years ago in an acid-trip haze and never bothered to send so much as a postcard.

Every time I see Annika since her return, conflicted feelings well up. Joy, yes, but also disappointment, and something unnamable.

I hover outside her door, my hand poised to knock, but I can hear the lilt of her German accent, worn soft by half a lifetime here, as she talks to someone. She laughs, and my heart pushes against my rib cage. She has been back for almost two weeks and I haven't had a moment alone with her.

I hear the low rumble of a male voice in the room with her, and my hand drops to my side. She already has a boyfriend, only two weeks home? Maybe it's just a friend, but this idea rings false as soon as I think it.

Annika is not the kind of woman men can be friends with. She's too beautiful.

In fact, Wolf's mother is the most beautiful woman I've ever seen. It's legendary, her beauty, the stuff of Greek myths.

When I was younger, in all my fantasies, she was *my* mother. Wolf was like my brother, only I wished he wasn't around at all, so I could have all of Annika's attention. I was greedy like that.

I still am.

She has her own private cabin at the north end of the village, which sat empty for the year she was gone. She is one of the original members of Sadhana, and such longevity comes with privileges. Also, Mahesh has a thing for her, I think. He will give Annika whatever she wants, including private cabins no one else can stay in, not even her own son.

So it disgusts me a little to think of some random dude in there with her, his body oil soiling her pristine sheets, his presence ruining any hope I had of an hour alone with her. I just wanted to ask her to have breakfast with me. Coffee, or tea. I wanted to ask her about rehab and tell her about my life and have her look at me like she cares that I'm alive.

I should know better than to want any of this, but I can't help myself.

I turn and start to walk away, when the lock on the door

clicks and the door swings open, startling me. Heat rushes to my face, as if I've been caught in the act of doing something wrong. It's the guy, some rumpled Rastafarian with dreadlocks down to his waist, a scruffy beard, and a T-shirt that reads, "I'm a soldjah in Jah army." There are pillow creases still on his cheek.

He blinks at me, and before I can hurry away, Annika steps into the doorway and sees me too.

"Laurel, *liebling*! What a surprise!"

"Oh hi," I say, my voice jittery.

"What are you doing here?" She smiles, perplexed.

"I . . . was just stopping to see if you'd had breakfast yet," I say, because I can't think of a lie.

"I haven't, no."

The Rastafarian leans in and kisses Annika hard on the lips. "I'm out," he says, no trace of a Jamaican accent, which makes his appearance seem like he's wearing a costume. "I'll leave you ladies to your morning."

He walks away, and suddenly I have what I wanted.

"I was just going to go over to the cafeteria. You want to come with?"

I hate how weak and hopeful my voice sounds.

She runs a hand over her long, blond hair and gives the idea a moment's thought. "How about I drive us to town for breakfast out?" she says. "That way we can have some peace and quiet."

This is more than I could have dared ask for. The cafeteria will be full of people who know Annika and will stop and talk to her, which means I will be lucky to get in ten minutes of alone time with her. But an entire ride to town and back, a sit-down breakfast where we look at menus and wait for our orders to arrive, then linger over our food and drinks?

Bliss.

"That would be awesome," I say, beaming. "It can be my treat!"

I have money from helping Pauly with his bike business, but she waves away this suggestion as if it's ridiculous. There have always been unconfirmed rumors of Annika having a massive trust fund. "Don't be silly. I'm buying. Just let me get myself pulled together."

In a few moments she emerges from the bathroom, dressed. She sweeps her long hair up into a messy bun and slides on a pair of sandals. She smiles at me.

"I'm so glad you stopped by," she says, and my disappointment vanishes.

She is my Annika again, exuding beauty like some rare species of animal.

We go to her car, a biodiesel Mercedes that's probably twice as old as I am and that smells of incense on the inside and french fries on the outside from the cooking oil it burns, and we ride to town talking about nothing much, small talk. Who has come and gone from the village, and so on. She tells me about traveling around Europe and Asia after her stint in rehab, but this is not what I want to talk to her about.

I have the panicked feeling that this time alone with her is being wasted, that it will pass without my ever getting a chance to say what I want to say.

I'm not even sure what I want to say.

I'm curious about her year away, but mostly I want her to

be curious about what's happened to me since she's been gone. I want to tell her my plans, and I want her to give me advice. Should I go to college? Travel? Keep working with Pauly?

I don't know. I need a crystal ball, or a parent, to tell me what to do.

The last option—working with Pauly—feels safest, but also is the most depressing. I have spent nearly my whole life at the village. I want to leave, but I have nowhere to go, no family to visit, no sense of how to be anywhere else in the world. Sometimes I imagine going off to find my parents, who will feel terrible for having left me here to be raised by strangers and who will then try to make it up to me. But I'm not even sure if they're alive, and if they are, I'm not really sure I want to know them.

I want Annika to take me by the hand and tell me what to do. Maybe tell me she will go with me on a trip to Europe, pay for the whole thing herself, show me the world I haven't seen yet, introduce me to her family as her daughter. This last bit, if I am being completely honest, is what I most want. What I could never ask for.

We go into a little restaurant that's known for its herbal teas and vegetarian breakfasts, and Annika glances at the menu before ordering a jasmine green tea and a Greek vegan scramble. I say I will have the same thing, though I would rather have something with cheese and bacon and lots of sour cream.

"So tell me," she says when the waitress leaves, "what have you been doing with yourself?"

Now, faced with this moment, I go blank. I don't know

what to tell her that will sound enticing enough to keep her interest.

I shrug stupidly. "Oh, you know, the usual. School, working with Pauly."

"Yes, the bike business—how is that going?"

"It's really taking off," I say. "My designs have been selling well."

"So you're designing and painting too?"

"I do a few designs, mostly Mehndi stuff Pauly doesn't have the patience for," I say.

Pauly's business, Art Bike, is pure genius, though I'd never tell him that. He gets old bikes with nice lines, restores them, and we give them artsy paint jobs, then sell them to trendy Bay Area bike shops. Pauly's style is more art deco–influenced, while I'm all about the intricate details.

"Any boyfriends in your life?"

"No."

"A pretty girl like you? You must have lots of interested guys."

I warm to the compliment but shrug again. I've never been into relationships, at least not serious ones. There are guys, yes, but what to say about someone I've slept with a few times but never want to spend time with in the light of day?

"I always thought you and Wolfie might end up together. Maybe not now, but eventually."

She pronounces his name "Volfie," with a soft German *V*.

"Oh god, no."

"Why is that so crazy? You know each other better than anyone else."

"That's the problem. No mystery."

This idea is nauseating to me, like thinking I will some-day marry my brother. I don't know how Annika can sug-gest it.

"Mystery is important," she says, nodding. "But I can't help wishing. I worry about that boy."

Wolf has grown strangely withdrawn and quiet these past few years. He has disappeared into himself, and I hardly see him anymore, but when I do, he's often alone. And silent.

"He's fine," I say, wanting to steer the conversation else-where, but I can't think what to talk about.

"He reminds me too much of his father now. I don't want him to go down that road."

By that road, I know she means suicide. Which Wolf's father committed the year we turned thirteen. I will never forget that detail, since it made me think that thirteen really is an unlucky number.

The waitress arrives and sets down on the table our cups of tea, along with a small jar of honey.

"Wolf would never do that," I say, unable to get out the words *commit suicide,* but I don't know if it's true.

The old happy-go-lucky Wolf wouldn't, anyway.

Annika smiles, but there is a sadness in her eyes I don't like. It's how she used to look when she needed a hit or a drink, or both.

Wolf exists in my earliest memories as a golden-brown sliver of a boy with gentle hands and watchful eyes. He seemed to have emerged from the soil beneath our feet—that was my childish impression of him. He was dirty, feral looking, a little animal that I felt like I'd managed to tame simply by sitting next to him. And his attention and friendship evoked the same feeling you get when a wild animal graces you with its trust: as if you are chosen.

I still feel that way about him, but he no longer chooses anyone as his trusted companion. Especially not me.

I was the one who first called him Wolfie, and later, Wolf, as if he were my own personal forest creature. Back then he was always Wolfgang, thanks to Annika's prehippie aspiration to be a concert pianist. It struck me even as a small child that it was a terrible name for him.

There was a time (when I was like five years old) when I thought we would always be together, that we would get married and have little golden-skinned babies and live happily ever after.

I don't think that anymore, of course.

I stopped believing in happily ever after long ago, in a land far, far away.

Our food arrives, faster than I would have expected, and when the waitress disappears, Annika smiles across the table at me. "Will you pray with me?"

I freeze, and my stomach drops.

I've heard the rumors—that Annika has gotten all Jesusy. It's the AA, people say in hushed whispers, which was apparently part of her rehab program. She's gone all in. But I didn't quite believe it.

She is reaching for my hand across the table, and I let her take it, not knowing what else to do.

She bows her head and closes her eyes, so I do the same, but I feel like a fraud. I've been raised around spirituality at Sadhana, but not this kind. Not religion, which I've only seen in movies about people living regular lives in regular American places.

Sadhana Village is not like any of those places. Mahesh's philosophy (he's the closest thing the village has to a guru, though he denies such titles and is an aging hippie with a gray ponytail and a passion for white pants) is loosely based on yogic principals, with a little Buddhism thrown in. Mother Earth is the only "god" and "walk in peace" the only prayer.

She is praying out loud, words I can't even register, words that don't sink in, because I am in shock. My beloved Annika, always so near the edge, always a shooting star blazing across my life, is a *Jesus freak*?

When she says amen I murmur the word myself, "Amen," because I think that's what I'm supposed to do.

But I don't have a clue what it means.

## NICOLE

When I wake up in my upstairs bedroom after our first night in my grandparents' old house, I am aware of the silence. I'd fallen asleep with my headphones on, music blaring, to block out the storm of my parents' argument, but at some point I must have pulled them off in my sleep, because all I hear now is nothing at all.

My parents are morning people, so it's never quiet in our house when the sun comes up. Mom is always making breakfast, putting away dishes, sweeping the floor. Dad, when he's home, is always hammering or building or fixing something.

The silence leaves me cold, though it's already stuffy and warm with the heat of the morning sun blazing in.


## WOLF

Try to imagine what a tree must love.

I'm not saying it will be easy to see things from the point of view of a tree. We don't even consider that trees might have points of view, but they do.

They absolutely do.

The tree wants life to flow through it. The tree wants to be an ecosystem for birds, insects, fungi, and other animals. It's not a conscious wanting. We are among the animals, so a tree that's strong and healthy and possessing the right shape is happy to hold a tree house.

This is what Mahesh told me when I was twelve and building my first treetop dwelling. I'd just learned about the importance of the tree's bark and was worried about damaging the bark of the tree I was working on. He helped me understand what a tree cares about and what it doesn't, what damage it can suffer for the sake of the greater good and what it can't.

This is not like that horrible children's book, *The Giving Tree*, where the tree gives everything and the human only takes and takes and takes. I'm talking about a more respectful and symbiotic relationship in which the tree is loved and revered for its beauty, strength, and grace.

I've started to worry not about the tree but about the sound of hammering nails, now that we have neighbors. What if the noise of nailing down roofing tiles leads them here, and what if they notice that my little tree house is built on their property?

My trespassing wasn't intentional. I chose the spot at first for the tree, a perfect black oak, which easily supports a house. Also it has a clear view through the forest to the east, of the sunrise and the mountains. It was only after I'd built the foundation structure in the tree that I noticed the few rotting fence posts that had once served as demarcation between properties. Sections of an old barbed wire fence still existed in spots along the property line, but so much of it was gone now that it was sometimes hard to tell where Sadhana's property ended and the neighboring property began.

Even after realizing my mistake, I figured no one would care, since the property wasn't occupied. Now I'm forced to finish the house while looking over my shoulder, worrying about who might discover what was meant to be a tiny fortress against the world, a place of complete solitude.

Foolish are the plans of mice and men, but trees never make foolish plans—or any plans at all.

I've come to think of building this house as a little prayer.

I've included lots of windows, partly because finding abandoned ones to salvage has been easier than finding enough siding to cover the outer walls. And also because I want to let in the forest and the light. But staying warm when it's cold will be a challenge. Hard to imagine being cold when it's this hot outside. Maybe this will only be a spring, summer, and fall house. It's too early to plan for the winter of my discontent.

I am just about to call it a day when a voice shocks me out of my skin.

"What are you doing?" I hear from below.

I spin around and look down to find the new girl, Nicole, standing next to my scrap woodpile, staring up at me.

"Putting a roof on," I say.

She takes in the strange tree house, its oddly placed windows and mishmash of colors. "What is this place?"

She is the first person to see it—the first person besides me to know of its existence. Now it can never be truly secret again.

I should feel intruded upon, maybe even angry, but I don't. I'm actually a little thrilled that she's here.

# Four

NICOLE

When I find the strangest guy I've ever met sitting on top of the strangest tree house I've ever seen, I get the unsettling sense that I've entered a dream. Does this guy ever hang out on solid ground?

I look around at the woods, confirming the fact that I am indeed awake. These are the woods I've been walking through, and I am still just as sweaty and thirsty as I was five minutes ago, looking for the creek my dad aimed me toward a half hour ago.

I watch as Wolf climbs down a ladder and comes closer. He looks a little wary, not quite like he was the first time I saw him. I get the sense that he doesn't want me here, though I couldn't say what gives me that feeling.

"Hi," he says. "Where's your gun?"

"I'm not hunting."

"So you don't carry it whenever you come into the woods,

just to be safe? You might run into a cute animal you want
to kill."

"I have a knife," I say, pulling it out of my back pocket to
show him. "You know, in case I see Bambi."

He can't tell if I'm being serious, and I don't smile to give
him any clues.

"What brought you out here?"

"I heard your hammering."

"You were just wandering around the woods alone?"

"Actually, I was looking for the creek my dad said was out
this way."

He points in the direction I was already heading.

"It's just down the hill, maybe ten minutes, but it's nearly
dry."

I will have to see for myself.

"Okay, well, thanks," I say, turning to go, ignoring the
strange urge I have to linger.

"Wait," he says, "If you want, I can show you where the
creek has a deeper pool. It's a little further, but if you want
to go for a swim—"

"No thanks," I say. "I can find it."

I don't correct his assumption that I'm off for a swim, because there's no point in explaining my father's insistence
that I know, like the back of my hand, where all local water
sources are.

He says nothing in response, but as I look at him I can't
seem to walk away. Our gazes linger a little too long on each
other, until I look away, pretending to survey the forest.

"Would you like a tour of the tree house?" he finally asks.
"It has a great view."

"Why are you building it all the way out here?"

"I guess you could say it's a temple of solitude."

I have no idea what to say to that. I don't know if he's serious or joking, so I say nothing. Maybe temples of solitude are a part of his weird religion.

He starts back up the ladder and motions for me to follow. I can't resist.

The interior is all unmatched old windows, unfinished plank floors and walls, a blank space—except for the feeling of forest all around, thanks to the many windows. It looks like someone got drunk and decided to build a tree house almost entirely out of salvaged windows still in their many-colored old wood frames.

"So what is this place for, really?"

He shrugs. "I just like to build things is all."

"Build things?"

I try to imagine any of the kids from my old high school going deep into the woods to build a bizarrely funky tree house just for the sheer pleasure of it. I try to imagine any of them standing here next to me now, shirtless and sweaty, hair pulled into a ponytail, wielding a hammer as if they've used it a thousand times.

I can't.

Not even the wood shop kids would have done something like this. There's a sort of mismatched beauty in the little house, like it's a sculpture in a museum rather than a place that serves a function.

"So how many tree houses have you built?"

He frowns. "I think this is the tenth or eleventh? I lost count."

"Where are the rest of them?"

I imagine them scattered throughout the woods, magical little houses waiting to be discovered by almost no one.

"Mostly on the Sadhana grounds in the main village. When it's warm enough, people stay in them, when they come for retreats and stuff."

"Wow."

"But this one I guess is just for me."

"All the way out here?"

"Out here I don't have to share it."

For the first time, I realize the problem. I'm pretty sure I was still on our property when I came across Wolf and his tree house. I'd been loosely following the property line as marked by the old fence, and I can see even now the posts that still mark where the missing section of fence used to be.

"This is on our property," I blurt, realizing too late that I'm again accusing him of trespassing, like some cranky, territorial hick.

All that's missing is my rifle.

His eyes widen. "Really?"

"Yeah, see the fence line down there?" I say as I point through a long, skinny window.

He looks. "Hmm. Do you think your parents will mind?"

"Probably."

Understatement of the year. My dad is all about property boundaries. He'll be furious when he sees this place.

He turns and points out the opposite window. "That view, and the solidness of this tree, are the reasons I chose this spot. I guess I wasn't thinking about property boundaries at the time."

"Maybe my dad won't find this place," I say, but I don't sound very convincing, and I'm not sure I want this guy squatting on our land either.

We don't know anything about him. Maybe he wants to grow pot here or something. How should I know?

"I'm sorry about the property line thing," he says, shrugging like it's no big deal.

The way he does it makes me wonder if he knew all along and just didn't care.

"Are you, like, planning to live here or something?"

He shrugs again. "You make it sound so formal. I don't have real specific plans, honestly."

"You've gone through a lot of trouble to build it," I point out.

For some reason he's started to irritate me, and I can't help prodding him.

"Don't worry, I'm not going to start throwing wild parties out here or anything. I guess I just wanted a place far away from everyone else, and hardly anyone has been in these woods besides me for years."

The weird intimacy of our aloneness starts to get to me. Kneeling here in this little space next to Wolf, I'm both drawn to him and repelled. He fascinates me, and I know he shouldn't.

"I have to go," I say. "My dad's going to wonder where I am."

I back up toward the ladder, suddenly shocked at myself that I'm here in this place, alone with a guy I don't know at all.

"Are you going to tell him about this?"

I look up at him as I start to descend the ladder. "No," I say, but I'm not sure if I mean it. "Not right now."

One thing is for sure: Dad doesn't need any more reasons to be stressed out right now.

I try to imagine where Mom is, what she's thinking. I don't know what it means that she's gone, but I know by the strain on Dad's face that it doesn't mean anything good.

I try to picture her going off on a short visit to her distant cousins in Fresno, then coming back once she's gotten used to the idea of living in the middle of nowhere. I can't, though. I just can't see her getting used to this place. None of us understood before we came here exactly how bad it is.

I don't know why it never occurred to Dad that she'd freak out. Maybe we've all been taking her for granted too much, though, assuming she'd be there no matter what. But looking back, I think of the distant look in her eyes, her distraction, her researching graduate schools, her rarely seen smile, and I realize we have all been kind of clueless.

And now that she's not here? Now what?

What if she never comes back?

Dad might be the person driving the car in our family, but Mom is the engine that makes it run, and a car isn't really a car without an engine.

I head off to the east, down the gentle slope of the hill, where fallen leaf matter and tree branches cover the earth. I am already getting used to walking through these woods, where so few trails exist except those traveled by deer and other animals. When I reach the bottom of the slope, I can see where a deep creek would run, if this past winter hadn't been so dry. There is only a shallow flow visible now. I fol-

low it over rough land for a while until I come to the pool
Wolf mentioned. It's maybe a foot or two deep, so I take off
my boots, roll up my jeans, and wade in to cool off.

The water here in the shade is cold. All water in these parts
is snowmelt from the Sierra Nevada, Dad made sure to in-
form me on the drive north. Mostly clean, good for drinking.

But there's not much of it to drink, if this is our closest
source.

California gets its rain in the winter, so a dry one means
no water for the rest of the year. In the desert, where we'd
lived since I was thirteen, we didn't notice the drought much,
since there's always a drought in the desert. I heard about it
on the news, though, and now we have to worry about how
we'll get any water at all.

I think of the wildfires that have been burning all over
California since spring. Dad sees them as a sign of the coming collapse of society, but I think they're just a sign of
drought.

Everything about our move here feels a little reckless, a
little wrong, and Mom's leaving seems like confirmation
of that.

Dad will come up with a plan, though. He always has a
plan.

On day two of my mother being gone, the movers delivering all of our stuff arrived late. Once they were finished unloading everything from the truck, we unpacked, while my
father stopped occasionally to stare out a window at the
empty driveway. He never said a word about Mom disappearing. If Izzy and I were a different kind of sisters, we

might have exchanged worried glances or talked about our missing parent, but instead she avoided my gaze when we passed in the hallway and spent most of the day in her room cleaning and arranging her stuff.

We have a strict system for unpacking after moves, which I thought would unravel without Mom present to do her part, but somehow Dad redistributes the responsibilities so that we are entirely unpacked and the house is as set up as it can be by ten o'clock that night.

On day three, Mom still didn't come back. Our house, its run-down appearance only emphasized by our normal suburban belongings, is depressing to look at. Dad's expression grew grim, and his silence had a weight to it.

On day four, he announces to me that we're making a trip to the grocery store. My sister stays behind while my dad and I get into his truck and ride in the same uncomfortable silence that has hovered between us for the past two days like a bad smell. But in the small space of the truck's cab, I can't stand it anymore.

"Where did Mom go?" I ask, the question barely squeaking out.

Dad's grip on the steering wheel tightens, and he stares straight ahead. "I don't know."

It's exactly what I was hoping he would not say.

"But didn't she say anything about where she was going, or when she's coming back?"

"No."

"What about her cell phone?" I say, but I already know it's turned off, because I've tried calling it from Izzy's phone.

"She left it at the house."

"Oh." That was typical Mom. She'd never adapted to the habit of taking her phone with her everywhere, and half the time she let the battery go dead, too, and then never noticed that it wasn't ringing.

"Have you tried calling any of her family?"

"A couple of times, but they haven't returned my calls."

"That seems like where she would go, don't you think?"

To this, he says nothing, and again I try to imagine my mom at this moment, where she is and what she's doing. I come up blank.

I have only ever imagined her being our mom the second grade teacher, doing mom and teacher things, living to take care of us and her students. Even the idea that she had dreams outside of this world just seemed like a vague concept, no more comprehensible or interesting than a calculus equation.

"You don't think she could be, like, hurt or something, do you?"

Silence again.

"Dad? This is serious. What if she wrecked her car, or got lost, or . . ."

Or what? I don't know.

"The police would have called if anything happened to her. She doesn't want to be found, is what I figure."

"But why?" I say stupidly.

I know exactly why she's left. I guess I just want to hear him say it.

"I don't know," he answers, his tone flat enough to let me know that this subject is finished.

My dad never admits he doesn't know something, and something about my world shifts a little when those words exit his mouth. I understand for the first time just how shaky the ground is beneath my feet. One thing I've always been able to count on is my dad's absolute self-assuredness, and the other is the fact of my parents being together.

I have no doubt that Dad loves Mom. His way of loving her might not be what she wants, but he still does. I'm sure of it. I'm not so sure, looking back, how she feels about him, though. I come up blank.

Out the window, pine forest blurs by. We again pass the large redwood sign with copper lettering that reads SADHANA VILLAGE AND SPIRITUAL RETREAT CENTER.

"What do they do at that Sadhana place?" I ask.

"They're a bunch of pagan wacko earth worshippers."

I glance over at him, at his jagged profile as he glares ahead at the road. He still keeps his dark hair in a buzz cut, even though he's retired now. He hadn't been planning to retire— it happened all of a sudden, without any explanation—and his haircut always gives me the feeling that he's going to put on his uniform and go back to work any day now. Then I look away again before he can catch me watching him.

*How do you know who they are?* is what I want to ask.

But what I say is, "Is it like a church or something?"

"It's probably a group of hippies using the words *spiritual retreat* as a front for a pot-growing farm."

I think of Wolf, the guy from the woods—not for the first time. He is so unsettling and odd, and no matter how hard my brain tries, there is not a category it can fit him into. He's the opposite of me that way, I think, because I fit perfectly into the categories I'm supposed to: obedient Asian daughter, straight-A nerd, expert marksman (thanks to my father's training), boring good girl.

I know how people see me as I sit obedient and silent in class, rarely raising my hand to give answers, always getting the answers right when asked. I know I am a stereotype to kids I've gone to school with, and it hasn't really bothered me.

"Let me make something clear," Dad says. "We're not on an army post anymore. People come in every shade of crazy out here in the civilian world, and it's your job to keep yourself separate, keep the outside world from getting in, you understand?"

"Who am I supposed to be friends with?"

"You don't need friends. You've got your sister, and that's plenty."

I roll my eyes at the trees outside the passenger window. The idea of Izzy being pals with me is so ridiculous that I wonder if our father has ever actually *met* my sister. I mean, I know he has, but *has* he?

"I'm not really Izzy's type of person," I say.

"Don't talk back. You and Izzy are family, and there's no such thing as not being each other's *type of person* when you're talking about your flesh and blood. You hear me?"

I stifle a sigh. "Yes, sir."

I have heard all this before, in various forms. It was stupid of me to start such a conversation, knowing it would lead straight to nowhere. Maybe because Izzy is so much more girlie than I am, he sees her as this incomprehensible and fragile creature, in need of a bodyguard.

He doesn't know her at all.

. . .

When we get back from the grocery store, I help Dad unload enough food to last at least a month. He works in grim silence, and I wonder if he'd been hoping to come home and find Mom back. In the kitchen, he has already assigned cabinets for each type of food, to be lined up in careful rows, so I do my best to put everything exactly in its place.

When I have nothing left but a giant bag of dried rice and no empty canisters in which to empty it, I look for Dad to ask him what he wants me to do with it. I know from past experience not to let it sit in a pantry and get infested with moths. After searching the house, I find him in his newly set-up office. He is flipping through the pages of a binder on his desk, then pausing to write something on a page.

"Um," I say to get his attention. "What should I do with the rice?"

He frowns up at me as if he hasn't understood the question, and the vague look in his eyes sends a jolt of fear through me. He never looks anything but self-assured. Now, though, he seems a little frail, and older than I've ever thought of him. I can see streaks of gray at his temples that I've never noticed before, and there are deep lines around his mouth and eyes.

I think of the way he's changed in recent years, the way his opinions have gotten more extreme, his actions less predictable, and I suppress a shudder.

"I'm going to be gone for a while," he says. "You'll be in charge here until I come back."

His words take a while to sink in, and I stare dumbly, unsure what to say.

He glances up at me from the binder, looking tired and distracted. "Well? Any questions?"

"Where are you going?"

"To find your mother."

"For how long?"

"For however long it takes to find her."

"So . . . me and Izzy are staying here?"

We don't even have phone or Internet service yet. It's all part of Dad's plan to live off the grid, but his envisioned solar power panels are nowhere near being installed. At least he bothered to turn on the electricity with the local power company for the time being. I guess I should be thankful for that.

"That's right. You've got enough food to last you, and I'll leave you with some cash and the hunting rifle."

"But—" slips out of my mouth before I can stop myself. It's my father's least favorite word.

He gives me a sharp look. "You'll be fine," he says, but I can't tell if he's trying to convince me or himself.

Questions crowd my thoughts, but before I can form any of them into words, my dad snaps shut the black binder and holds it out to me. I can see now it's the household binder, which contains every detail he considers necessary for the proper running of our family. It's a strange document he created for my mom, my sister, and I years ago, which we never look at unless forced to but that he refers to at any opportunity.

I take the binder, the weight of it awkward in my hands, and clutch it to my chest as if I am drowning and it will keep me afloat.

Me and Izzy alone in this broken-down house, in the middle of nowhere, does not sound like a good idea. But this is another one of his challenges, I know. He wants me to prove I can do it. He wants me to show that I can survive, no matter what the circumstances.

I stare out the window beyond his desk, as if I might find some answers there, written in the sky. I can think of a million reasons him leaving us here to go look for Mom is a bad idea, but then, I know he can't just sit around waiting, either. It's not his style.

"Where will you look?" I finally ask.

"That's not for you to worry about." He squints at me as if I'm slow-witted.

More questions occur, like how will we get in touch if something happens? Dad doesn't have a cell phone, because he believes they're unnecessary crutches and make it too easy for the government to track our every move, and being the good daughter I am, I opted not to get one, either. Izzy has a cell phone, but the reception here only works occasionally, if she goes and stands outside in the driveway, and even then it's weak and spotty.

"You two keep working through the chore list," he says. "With any luck I'll be back in a few days or a week."

With any luck. I try to imagine keeping Izzy out of trouble for a whole week. I guess it's possible, since we live so far from everything, but how will I survive a week alone with her?

Or more than a week?

I can't let myself ponder that.

My father is not the kind of man you argue with when you are his daughter. He is so sure of his own rightness that any voice to suggest otherwise is as comprehensible and convincing to him as a fly buzzing around his head. It is no more than an irritant to be swatted away, or preferably, crushed.

I have known this for as long as I can remember, though it's only recently become an idea I can put into words.

"Where's Isabel?" he says, brushing past the desk and picking up, I notice only now, a suitcase that has been sitting next to the door.

"In her room, I think."

"Isabel," he yells into the hallway. "Get down here."

Izzy comes slinking down the stairs, her feet clad in purple thong sandals, her denim shorts and tank top just this side of too skimpy on her newly curvy body to pass Dad's approval.

She blinks at us but says nothing.

"I'm going to look for your mother. Your sister's in charge while I'm gone. You're to do whatever she says, you understand?"

Izzy's mouth opens, her expression horrified. "What?"

"You heard me. I don't want any sass."

"I want to go too," she says.

"You're staying here to get the house fixed up. You've got a chore list to work through so when your mother and I get back everything's ready for her."

I can't imagine what he means by getting the house fixed

up. Are we supposed to ignore the stains on the walls and ceiling, the broken, duct-taped windows, the creepy haunted house vibe, and just set up housekeeping as if this place is normal? Or are we supposed to pull out our nonexistent handyman skills and fix everything?

He explains nothing. Instead he says, "All right then," and walks down the hall and out the front door, suitcase in hand.

Izzy and I follow behind, dumbstruck.

I stand on the front porch and watch him drive away, his truck leaving a cloud of dust on the parched gravel road, and I keep thinking he will change his mind, realize how crazy it is to leave two teenage girls alone in the wilderness for however long he's going to be gone. But then, when has he ever changed his mind about anything?

Pretty much never.

I turn and see the expression on Izzy's face. Already, I suspect, she is imagining the vast possibilities for trouble she can get into with her newfound freedom.

"We're staying right here," I say, which is kind of ridiculous, since we don't have a car to go anywhere and we're probably five miles from town.

Where would we even go?

She shrugs. "Suit yourself, but if we're here alone? I'm going to find out what people do for fun around here."

"No, you're not. You're going to stay here like Dad said and help me."

I realize I sound like the biggest dork on earth, but what else am I going to say?

The truth is, I really have no idea how to control Izzy. For her entire life, she's been this hurricane force I have to live with, always wary of what havoc she might wreak.

She rolls her eyes. "Whatever."

"Not whatever. If you don't do what Dad said, I'll be sure to let him know exactly how you behaved while he was gone."

"You tell Dad and I'll make sure you live to regret it," she says in a fake-sweet voice, then turns and walks back inside.

For the first time, I miss Mom. We are not the closest mother and daughter pair, and I know I disappoint her by taking my father's side, but still. How could she have left us here like this, with no explanation, no good-bye—nothing?

My fingers itch for my journal and a pen, because I want to write out this riddle, put it on paper, where I can arrange and rearrange my thoughts until they start to make sense. I guess I got the writing habit from my dad, the doomsday author, though he doesn't even know I keep a personal journal, aside from the survival skills notebook he makes me keep. It's my one rebellion, the only place I can say what I want without his approval.

I have never been good at getting inside my mother's head. Some things about her are so familiar—her warm jasmine scent, her voice, her wide cheekbones—and some are as foreign to me as if she is an alien being. My mother is not the type to talk about her feelings, or her past, or anything about herself, really. She issues orders, asks us about our day, explains how to do things. But she herself is a closed book, I realize.

But now I have to wonder about this other side of my mother, the one willing to pick up and leave without saying good-bye, the one who is, unlike me, brave enough to stand up to my father. Maly is my mother's name, and for the first time in my life, I see that she is a whole separate person who is not just a mother. The side of her we've been oblivious to all this time, the side with hopes and dreams and interests that have nothing to do with our family, is the side I'm starting to wish I knew.

Maly, I think, is possibly a more complicated person than any of us noticed.

When I realize I'm still clutching Dad's household binder, I fling it to the ground and go inside.

# PART TWO

# You're on Your Own

Every prepper fantasizes about being put to the test. There is no point in prepping if you don't really believe the world is going to end, right? There is always the fantasy of the heroic deeds, the adventure, the feeling of living on the edge. I see this in all the prepping magazines my dad leaves lying around the house, the websites and message boards he leaves open on the computer.

But I've always wondered about this fantasy and its potential for disappointment. After all, if we really want to live like that, why not pack up and move to the far reaches of Alaska right now? Why wait?

And I see, this is exactly what my dad finally did. He's saying to us, and to the rest of the world, why wait? Why not start surviving the apocalypse now?

# Five

---

WOLF

I have been dreaming of the girl from the woods, Nicole. Although I don't normally remember my dreams, I remember this one clearly because I've had some version of it every night since I met her. She is stalking me in the woods, and after she shoots me in the leg and bends over me to see if I'm still alive, I kiss her.

It's not a complicated dream, but it is a vivid one, and it makes me want to see her again for reasons I'd rather not explain to myself. I wake up from it sweating, dry-mouthed, heart racing, weirdly aroused, and fearful at the same time.

I tell myself it's the recurring dream that keeps her in my thoughts, because I don't want to think about that strange girl with the gun. I don't want my mind to be full of nothing but her, the way it threatens to become. It goes against my Thoreaulike aspirations of simplicity and solitude. Henry never mentioned having girl crushes during his time at Walden Pond.

I am doing afternoon kitchen duty—and enjoying the rhythm of it—when Laurel finds me chopping vegetables for dinner. I like to chop, and even though my current task is dicing onions, my eyes are unaffected by them. Light slants in through the windows over the counter, and it glints off the chef's knife as it moves.

"You," she says, leaning against the butcher-block counter next to me and crossing her arms over her chest. "Where have you been?"

"For the last hour, here."

"I mean, like, all the time. You're on another planet." I look up at her for a moment, catch the pout in her eyes that she's kept out of her voice.

Laurel is a high-maintenance friend. She always wants more than I can give. I used to try to please her, used to like the way she seemed to need me, but I've learned the hard way not to.

"I've been here and there."

An irritated silence follows as she watches me chop. I'm good at it, and the white flesh of the onion quickly dissembles into a pile of quarter-inch cubes. Then I grab another and start the process again.

"I had a talk with Annika," she says.

I say nothing. I don't want to talk about my mother or anything else. I come early to kitchen duty so that I can work alone, without the noise of other people's chatter.

"She says she's worried about you."

"Hmm" is the sound I make.

I mean it to sound bored, to discourage her from further comment, but she interprets it as an invitation to say more, I guess.

"She thinks you're suicidal, like your dad."

If I didn't know Laurel so well, I might interpret this comment as some attempt at helpfulness. Or kindness.

But we have grown up together like trees intertwined at the trunk.

Siamese twins of parental neglect.

"She shouldn't worry," I say to the pile of onions.

"I worry too. You're acting depressed."

"I'm not."

She places a cold hand on my arm that's doing the chopping. I pause and look at her. Her blond hair is caught in a green batik cloth and hangs over one shoulder almost to her waist, and her gray-blue eyes reveal nothing. In her left nostril glints an ever-present silver ring.

"She told me she wants you to go with her to an AA meeting."

"I don't drink."

"She means as her family support person, or whatever."

It's not like Laurel to play intermediary between my mother and me, but then, nothing is normal about Annika since she came back. Maybe she really did instigate this.

"Why don't *you* go for me?" I offer, and go back to my chopping.

"She wants you, not me."

"Then why isn't she asking me herself?"

"She thought you might be more willing if I asked you. She thinks you're mad at her for being gone so long."

I say nothing.

"She made me *pray* with her," Laurel says, as if this is some kind of scandal.

"We live at a spiritual retreat center, in case you haven't noticed."

"No, this was like . . . praying to *Jesus*."

I am trying to decide what to say to that when the subject of our conversation walks through the kitchen door, which jingles every time someone opens it.

Beside me, Laurel goes deathly pale, probably worried my mother overheard her last comment.

"My two favorite people!" Annika says, seemingly oblivious. "Just the ones I was looking for."

I focus again on my chopping, as if it will deliver me from this place, but Annika sweeps in close and I can smell her beeswax scent.

"Did you ask him already?" she says to Laurel.

"Yes. He's being noncommittal."

"I was afraid of that. I realized it's really my job to convince him, isn't it?"

Laurel stares daggers at me, but I have no idea why.

"Darling," Annika says. "It's family night at my recovery group tonight at six. I need you there."

I drop the knife onto the counter, pick up the heavy oak cutting board, and brush the huge pile of onions into a bowl for the cooks who will be here shortly.

But this kitchen is already way too crowded.

I stalk to the back door without saying a word and leave, not taking the time to wash the onion scent off my hands, banking on the hope that my mother is too proud to follow after me, begging. That's why she sent Laurel in the first place, probably. But I have misjudged her, and she does follow, running to catch up with me. At least she is alone now when she stops me in front of the yoga center entrance.

"Wolf, just hear me out."

"I'm busy," I say. "What do you want?"

She tilts her head to the side, squinting her eyes at me. "What are you up to these days that has you so busy?"

I shrug, not willing to tell anyone here, and especially not her, about the new tree house.

"You are almost grown up," she says. "I want to spend time with you before you've gone off living your own life."

Now she wants to spend time with me. I choose not to point out that, for most of the past seventeen years, spending time with her son has been the last thing on her mind.

*It's a little late for that,* is what I feel like saying, but I don't. Silence is often the best strategy. It's hard to argue with.

"What? You think you can stonewall me?" she says.

"No," I say, edging my way toward the barn, where my bike and its trailer full of roofing material is parked. I've managed to convince anyone who ever asks that I have been hauling discarded wood and stuff that I find on our property to a guy in town who builds chicken coops with recycled materials.

But she reaches out and grabs my arm as I try to slip past.

"Wolfie, please."

"Please what?"

"I don't ask you for many things. Go with me, just tonight, okay? I need you there."

The thing I hate most about myself is that I want to feel needed. I especially want to feel needed by my mother. I don't want it with my brain, not with the part of myself that understands logic and reason. I want it with some primitive, lizard part of myself, deep down where logic and reason don't count for shit.

My chest gets this crushed-in feeling, and at the same time that I want to wrench my arm free and run, I stay there. I don't say yes, but she knows she has me.

"Meet me in the parking lot around five thirty, okay?"

She gives my arm a motherly squeeze, and she looks, for once, vulnerable. I nod and finally break free.

Giving up the idea of escape on my bike, I cross the grounds toward the woods, and soon I am in the shade and protection of the trees, where I know my way better than probably anyone else. I follow trails so faint only the deer know they exist, and I go deeper and deeper into the woods.

My mother will say she is a recovering addict. She will say she is sober (she loves to use the word *sober*, like it's a ticket to forgiveness for all past sins). But the only relevant thing is that she is an addict.

I can't remember a time before this was the most important fact about her.

I have the misfortune of being her only child, so whenever she decides she's going to get back on the motherhood bandwagon she directs all her misguided energy at me. This has led to a lifetime of unfortunate childhood memories. Like the time when I was twelve and she baked weed-laced brownies for my birthday party, and all my friends got either really high or really sick.

Or when I was nine and she drove me and Laurel and Pauly to the movies in town, but then she forgot about us and we spent half the night looking for her car, only to find it sometime after midnight parked outside a bar, her in the back seat making out with some guy.

My least favorite memory, though, is from the time right after my dad left us. I was six and Annika was alternating between depressive, drunken benders and periods of remorse when she felt the need to make sure I was okay. I was attending a Waldorf school at the time, since it was before the village school got started, and she showed up at school early to pick me up, for some reason I can't recall now. But she was drunk or high or something, and after she'd come stumbling into the classroom to get me, the teacher refused to let us leave, with her so clearly unfit to drive. So Annika threw a raging tantrum right there in front of all the other kids who'd been in the middle of doing finger painting, and I was standing there with my blue-stained fingers, watching my mother fall apart, until the police came and we had to ride in the back of the police car back to the village.

Every time I see a police car, I think of my mother, that horrible day, and my half-finished finger painting of a sunflower against a royal blue sky. I wish I still had that painting, so I could burn it.

Since returning from rehab, though, she is different in some way I find more disturbing than reassuring. She has a higher power, and she is taking things one day at a time, and she has given herself over to God-with-a-capital-G. Even Mahesh doesn't dare to question her on this.

Being a woman like Annika, who was raised by her

university professor parents in Heidelberg to believe in science and literature, to be skeptical of everything, to value learning above all else, I guess this is the kind of rebellion she is drawn to, first with her commitment to Sadhana Village and now with this—the rebellion into that which cannot be proven or disproven.

Faith.

I wish I could have some kind of faith in her, but I don't.

I don't know how much time has passed, since the following of deer trails has become a meditation, but I realize with a start that I've led myself back to the edge of the woods that look out on the house where Nicole is living. There are no cars parked there now, but I can see her outside, dragging a piece of lumber across the yard toward the old garden and orchard.

I squat against a tree trunk, amid the faint, musty smell of decaying leaves, and I watch.

I don't know why I watch, but the bad feelings from the dream that's been dogging me begin to fade and she takes shape as a real person again, her hands in work gloves as she pauses to brush sweat from her brow with a forearm. She moves again with that same unconscious grace I first noticed about her.

I see that, at least in this way, as she stacks one piece of lumber on top of another—building a raised bed, maybe— she is like me. We are both building something. She is not afraid of toil and sweat and dirt.

It would be wrong to stay here watching like a predator, when she is alone and going about her day. I should either go to her and offer to help with whatever it is she's doing or leave.

So I turn and head back into the woods, resisting the magnetic pull of her presence.

Choosing solitude, because it's safer.


We take the old Mercedes to town, its leather seats one of the more vivid memories of my childhood. My mother has always been a sketchy driver, so I insist on driving. Since it was my car during her absence, it should be a comfortable position—me in the driver's seat—but I mostly kept it parked because I prefer my bike, and I feel as if I have a dangerous animal in the seat next to me. This is the first time I've been really alone with Annika for any length of time since she came back.

It's awkward, at best.

I try to focus on the road while she tries to make up for a year in fifteen minutes, rambling on and on about her many revelations during therapy, most of which involve her feelings toward her mother, her anger at my father, her ambivalence about sobriety.

She says it all like it's a news flash, but I've heard it before. She's a broken record of recovery and relapse, only this time she seems totally convinced it's going to work.

As if, at the age of forty-three, all her past habits have been erased.

Maybe I sound bitter.

That's because I am.

I sit through the AA meeting, and when Annika talks,

introduces me, I realize she's building a new identity. Responsible Annika. Cleaned Up Annika. Jesusy Annika.

It makes me sick to my stomach, because it all feels like a lie she's asking me to tell with her—even my presence is a part of the lie.

Later we pull out of the lot of a low-slung community center that's painted a color somewhere between beige and yellow, a cinder block construction of the sort that doesn't even try to be anything but ugly.

I notice these things because I love to think about the shapes and lines of structures, how form and function intertwine, the purpose of one style or another, the ways utility and beauty come together—or don't, in this case.

I feel as if the smells of old coffee and cigarette smoke from the meeting have permeated my very being, after an hour in that place.

"So tell me what's been going on with you?" Annika asks me on the drive back home.

I grip the steering wheel and stare straight ahead, my mind blank. I don't think my mother has ever in her life before today wondered what's going on with me. Again I think, *Why now?*

It's too late for mother-son bonding of this variety.

I shrug. "Not much."

"You're gone from the house a lot. There must be something."

"Just doing deliveries, that's all. . . . Why do you care?" I say, perversely not wanting to tell her what she hopes to hear.

"I just want a better life for you than I had."

Which is a joke. She had a great childhood, with loving parents who gave her every advantage.

"Maybe you should have thought of that seventeen years ago," I say before I can stop myself.

For a few silent moments, the accusation hangs in the air between us. I don't look at her, don't want to see how she feels about it.

"You're angry with me," she finally says.

"Not really."

"I understand. You have the right to be angry. I just hope you can move past it and have some compassion eventually as well."

I roll a bitter response around on my tongue, weighing it, daring myself to say more, but I don't. I know she likes to argue. I don't want to give her that satisfaction.

"You've grown up so much this past year, but you're still my child. I still get to be your mother, whether you like it or not."

"You might want to read a how-to book."

She sighs, and I can see out the corner of my eye that she's staring straight ahead.

I used to ache for her attention, used to try my best to be a good kid, to do whatever she needed so that she'd notice me or love me or both. I don't really care so much anymore, and I'm not sure when the change happened. Definitely before she left, last year. Probably it happened sometime around when I hit puberty and realized the world is mostly a brutal place where we all have to take care of ourselves.

I turn the car off the main road and onto the gravel road

that winds through the woods to the village. I am focused on dodging potholes, because the road hasn't been repaired since who knows when.

"What do you want to do with your life?" she asks.

This is way too much parenting for one day. I don't want to answer, but I know she'll keep asking, so I shrug and say I don't know.

"Surely you have some ideas. Are you going to become the recycled building materials delivery man for the whole county?"

The truth is, I used to have answers to her question, but they've become obscured by the gray cloud that veils my thoughts lately. I can no longer imagine the future beyond my tree house or what it might bring.

"You were always so bright. College maybe?"

My mother attended a few years of college before dropping out and traveling around the world with my father. I suppose it was as good a way as any to spend those years, except she seems to have learned nothing, gained nothing, from the time spent. She has no real appreciation beyond the superficial for other cultures, no wisdom gained from a wider perspective on the world, and mostly I think it was just an excuse to try drugs from exotic places. It was her opium period, is what my dad used to say.

When I say nothing to her suggestion of college, she sighs again. "I really think you need therapy to get over your father's death, if you want to know the truth."

Now she's playing dirty. She's digging for a response, and I can't help myself. I give her one.

"Fuck you," I say. "Fuck therapy. It's never done you any good."

"That's not true," she says, choosing to ignore my insults. "I've grown a great deal from the work I've done."

I love how she calls it "work," as if at the end of a session in her therapist's office her back hurts and she has a paycheck in her hand. I'm sure it helps her feel like a useful human being, when she is, in fact, useless.

This is the problem with my mother—she has never even tried to be useful. She has always thought being beautiful is enough.

# Six

---

ISABEL

I am finally going to get out of this craphole.

For the past five days I've been stuck here, bored out of my mind, watching the paint peel off the walls while Nic runs around hammering things and planting things and acting like we're living in that show *Little House on the Prairie* Dad used to make us watch when we asked for TV time.

For a while I wasn't sure how long it would take to walk to town, or even which way to go to get there, but then I realized: hitchhiking. I can totally do that. I'll just have to be careful about who I stick my thumb out to. Like no creepy-looking dudes, no serial killers, and so on.

All I have to do is walk to the main road, hitch a ride, and I can be hundreds of miles away from here in a matter of hours.

The only thing that's been stopping me is the idea that Mom might come back home any time now.

Any *minute* now. . . .

But after almost a week? I'm sick of waiting.

And there is my sister, working like a slave in this unbelievable heat, hammering pieces of wood together to build raised beds, pulling weeds, turning the dirt with a hoe for reasons I cannot begin to imagine.

She tries to get me to help, but there is just no way.

Not a chance.

Yesterday morning I found a reclining lawn chair in our stuff in the barn, and I found a beach towel in the bathroom, and I found my forbidden bikini hidden in the bottom of my dresser drawer. Then I sat reading a contraband *Cosmo* magazine all afternoon from my mother's stash. We teens are totally not allowed to read magazines, unless we found one with a title like *Prairie Home Teen Canning Journal,* but Dad has never been able to convince our mother of the evils of pop culture.

Which maybe is why she's gone.

From the one spot on the driveway where my phone works exactly 10 percent of the time, I have sent her, like, fifty text messages since she left, but I don't know if she's read any of them yet. They say things like:

"Where did you go?"

"When are you coming back?"

"You have to come back. Dad is being crazy."

"Why haven't you answered me?"

"Dad left us here by ourselves. I'm going to call child protective services if you don't come back RIGHT NOW!!!!!!"

And so on.

I didn't really mean that last message, because while I can

maybe use the threat once or twice to get Nic to leave me alone, I know if I call CPS I will end up having to live in some gross home for teens or a foster home or something, and I'll probably get sexually abused, because that kind of thing always happens in those places.

For a while I considered taking the risk just so I could have some decent air-conditioning and TV and normal food, but then I decided it wouldn't be worth it.

No, I have to find Mom.

She's the only one in this crazy family who understands me, which is why I am extra confused that she would leave without taking me with her. She *knows* how much I hate this place.

I am totally (mostly) convinced she will be back sooner or later. Not that anyone has asked my opinion, but I'm pretty sure she just went for an extended spa visit and maybe some hard-core shopping while she considers her options for how to get our family out of this nightmare.

Probably she is thinking divorce, which really wouldn't be the end of the world.

I mean, living in this place is the end of the world as I care to know it.

I guess the sucky part would be that I'd have to go to my dad's house on some weekends to visit him, but the good part is a lot of Mom's family lives in Southern California—Long Beach, Newport Beach, Huntington Beach (all towns with the word *beach* in the name)—so we could move to the beach with her and not have to pretend we are mousy church girls anymore. We could stay with the cousins until we find our own place, which would definitely be a cool condo with a view of the ocean, and we could eat out every night and never have to can things again.

Maybe she's picking out our house now.

I get a little stab of guilt at this thought. I love my dad and all, and I don't totally want them to get divorced, but he so needs to take a chill pill on the crazy survival stuff. And he's not the perfect guy he pretends to be, anyway.

I am wrapping up my second day of sunning myself, having read all the *Cosmo* magazines I can find, when Nicole comes trudging back from the barn, sweaty and covered in filth.

This causes me to check my nails, which are currently painted an amazing shade of metallic orange that looks super pretty with my skin, and notice that I need to apply a touch-up coat tonight.

"Did you start dinner?" she asks me.

"No."

She turns and walks toward the house, her bony shoulders slumped, and I almost feel guilty. Nic is so hard to like, and we have nothing in common, but she's, like, the only person I've seen in days. I guess I should try to get along with her or something.

I make little resolutions to be nicer to her all the time, but they never last longer than an hour or two (well, I mean, they could last all day if I don't see her, but the second we start talking and stuff I suddenly can't remember why I wanted to be nice).

She's so irritating. She's like our dad's brainwashed robot.

But she knows how to cook way better than I do.

If I'm nice to her she might make something like chocolate chip cookies for dessert, and I'm getting hungry and sick of eating PBJs for every meal.

The sun has dipped below the tops of the trees and I am sitting in the shade now anyway, so I get up and follow her into the house while thinking of ways I can get on Nic's good side. I could check Dad's chore list and do one of the less hideous things on it. Or I could do something that would benefit me and try to scrub that nasty bathtub clean so I can take a bath later.

I'll do both. Chore list first, then bathtub. That way she can make cookies while I soak in the clean tub.

But inside the house I hear an awful groaning sound coming from the walls, like the house itself is in pain. I follow the sound down the hallway and into the bathroom, where Nicole is staring at the bathtub faucet, watching it as nothing comes out.

"What is that sound?" I ask.

"The pipes?" she says.

Like I would know.

"Oh my god. What's the matter with them?"

She breathes a ragged sigh. "No water, see?" She demonstrates by turning the faucet on and off, on and off. "I think it's air in the pipes that's causing the sound."

Horror balloons in my belly.

No *water*?

I have been baking in the sun all day and I smell like tanning lotion and sweat. I have to bathe or I am going to seriously freak out.

"So we just call the water company or whatever and have them come fix it, right?"

She sits down on the edge of the tub and stares at me. "We don't have water service here. We just have our own well."

"A *well*? You mean like with a bucket that we lower down on a rope?"

"No, not like that. It's . . . I don't even know how it works."

"Then we have to call someone who does. I'm not going to live without water."

She sticks her thumb in her mouth to gnaw on a nail, but no sooner does she have it between her teeth than she realizes what she's doing and sticks her hand between her legs. Our parents have forbidden her nail biting for so many years, she never does it in public. But it's easy to see she's still a nail-biter by all her ugly, bitten-down nails.

"We can't call anyone even if we could get your phone to work. We don't have enough money to pay them, and if anyone finds out we're out here alone, we could get Mom and Dad in trouble."

"We just say our parents are out for a little while."

"It might be something that takes days to fix, and like I said, we don't have enough money to pay a repairman."

I'm so sick of her acting like this, like she can't think for herself, that I want to grab her and shake her, but she's taller and stronger than me, so instead I go to the kitchen, where I saw a local phone book sitting on the counter. I start to flip through it when I realize I have no idea what to look up.

*Well repairman?* There isn't anything like that in the W section.

Nicole follows me into the kitchen and grabs the book. "Stop it," she says. "You have to let me think. Maybe I can figure out how to fix it myself."

"You're an idiot," I say, mostly because I'm mad and not because it's true.

I go to my room and dig around until I find my stash of birthday money. I have almost two hundred dollars I've been saving, which I have no intention of telling Nicole about because she'll want to spend it on something stupid like economy-size bags of beans. But I could take ten dollars and hitchhike to town and buy myself some dinner.

I look gross, so I wipe the sweat smell off as best I can with some facial cleansing wipes I have in my cosmetic bag, and I pull my hair back in a fresh ponytail and put on my favorite baseball cap. Then some fresh clothes and I almost look normal. I put on some deodorant and a spritz of the body spray my mom bought me for Christmas, even though Dad forbids us from wearing perfume, and I smell pretty normal, too.

I can hardly believe I finally have some real freedom for the first time in my life and I can't even take a shower before enjoying it. One thing's for sure, though—I'm not letting it go to waste.

When Nicole isn't looking I slip out the front door, ease the creaky screen door shut silently, and head for town while it's still light out.


## LAUREL

I am riding in Pauly's van with Pauly and Kiva when we spot the girl on the side of the road, her thumb stuck out half-heartedly, like she isn't really sure if she wants someone to pick her up. She is young and pretty, maybe early teens, with a body that guys like Kiva find as distracting as shiny objects.

"What have we here?" Kiva says as Pauly slows down and pulls to the side of the road where gravel meets grass.

I roll down the window. "Want a ride?"

She forces a smile. "I'm going into town, if you're headed that way."

"It's your lucky day."

Kiva leans over and opens the rear door on her side for her, and I already know the scenario that's going to play out. He's going to do everything he can to get in her pants, and unless she's got an iron will, he will succeed. He is, at the fully pubescent age of sixteen, ridiculously determined to put himself as far from virginity in the shortest amount of time he can manage.

This girl, though, she looks fresh. Untouched. Close up, I'd guess she's fourteen years old.

I catch a scent of some kind of fake raspberry stuff when she gets into the car, and when I turn to look at her I realize she resembles one of the new girls Wolf described. Same olive skin, same dark, straight hair, same vaguely Asian features.

"What's your name?" I ask.

"Isabel," she says.

"I'm Laurel, and this is Pauly," I say, nodding toward him.

"I'm Kiva," Kiva says from the backseat.

"Thanks for picking me up."

"Didn't your parents tell you never to hitchhike?" Pauly asks, peering at her in the rearview mirror, his tone slightly flirtatious even though he's totally, one hundred percent gay.

She shrugs. "Probably."

"You must be new around here, or I'd recognize you," Kiva says.

"I'm just here temporarily. Do you guys go to the high school here?"

"Not exactly," I say. "There's a school at Sadhana Village that we attend."

"I'm a graduate of the school of life," says Pauly.

"I'm studying the art of being," says Kiva, which is pretty much true for him. I haven't seen him crack open a book any time in recent memory.

"We decide for ourselves what we're going to study at the World Peace School."

"The World Peace School? Is that really what it's called?"

"Yep."

"You guys all live together?" the girl asks.

"Something like that," Pauly says. "You should come over and see our place. It'll blow your mind."

I refrain from an eye roll. I don't know what about a bunch of hippies in dorms and cabins is supposed to impress anyone, but I've lived there almost my whole life, so I guess I'm a bit jaded. I know what the village is, and what it isn't. I know it has never lived up to the spiritual ideals it was founded on, and I don't really care about that anyway, but I hate when people talk about it like it's some kind of super-special paradise.

Mostly it's a place where people escape from reality. And it's kind of a shitty place to grow up. I knew all about sex by the time I was, like, six years old, because I'd seen so many drugged-out losers doing it right out in the open, and I'd experienced a lot more than that by the time I was this girl's age. The stories I could tell her. . . . I mean, some of the people at Sadhana really are trying to be enlightened beings and all, but it also draws a lot of oddballs and people who don't want to live in the real world with real responsibilities.

Not that I blame them.

Pauly's favorite Queen song has come on the radio, and he has cranked up the volume so loud no one can talk. The music makes him drive faster, and as we speed toward town we can see billowing smoke over the mountains in the distance, from the nearest wildfires. It's been forever since a fire has gotten this close to us, but they come every year to this part of the state, as regular as the seasons. It's usually so hot and dry in the Sierras by this time of year that there's no stopping the flames.

I like how they make the night glow red sometimes, and I like how the smoke hangs in the valleys and colors the air beige. It feels like the end of the world.

Which reminds me of what Wolf told me about seeing the girl in the woods with the gun. I lean forward and turn down the radio as we reach the edge of town.

"So, do you have your own rifle?" I ask Isabel, and Kiva's eyebrows shoot up.

Isabel makes a disgusted face. "My sister does. Not me."

"Is your family into survivalism?"

She makes a pained face. "Um, my dad is, kind of, I guess."

I see from the tension in her mouth that I've caught her off guard, bringing up something she doesn't want to talk about.

"Seriously? You're a survivalist?" Pauly says.

"Do you guys believe the zombie apocalypse is coming?" asks Kiva, who loves zombies.

I don't understand how anyone loves zombies.

"No way. But my dad is kind of into that stuff, and my sister too. He's got her totally brainwashed."

Survivalist gun nuts, moving in right next door to our peace and love spiritual commune? It's such an awesome co-incidence I almost laugh out loud. I really have to meet the gun-toting sister, ASAP, and figure out what her deal is.

## NICOLE

When I realize Isabel is missing I try not to freak out. I mean, how far could she really go, anyway? She has no sense of direction and no money. But then I imagine her hitch-hiking, getting picked up by some creepy guy, and panic rises in my chest. Dad trusted me to be able to take care of my sister, the house—everything—and it's all falling apart. I've already failed, in less than a week.

I first search the property, hoping to find her moping in the barn or looking for something in the garage, or most unlikely of all, communing with nature outside, but part of me knows it's a fruitless search. I can tell by the silence, the peaceful stillness that Izzy is incapable of, that I'm alone. She is forever humming or fidgeting or declaring herself bored.

I think of my bike in the garage and go get it out. Maybe I can catch up to her before she gets picked up, if I ride fast. I am strapping on my helmet when I notice I have two flat tires. Of course. The bike has been sitting unused while we were getting ready to move and then moving. I am the only one in the family who owns a bike. My sister had one, but she left it unlocked at school and it was stolen last year, causing my dad to refuse to buy her another.

I look around for the tire pump but all I see are boxes waiting to be unpacked, because Dad doesn't include unpacking the outdoor stuff in our one-day unpacking frenzy schedule. And he didn't consider, in his rush to leave, that I might need to chase my sister down by bike. I mutter some curses, take off my helmet, and resign myself to running on foot after her.

And then I think, what if I don't? What if I just let her figure out on her own that it's a bad idea to take off like this? I still have the not-so-small issue of our lack of water to figure out.

Probably she will come back on her own. Probably I am worried about nothing.

Probably.

I decide to take the risk.

# Seven

---

WOLF

When I was very small it's possible that I loved Laurel. I don't remember a time when she wasn't in my life, but I do remember a time when she was at my side always, when we were best friends and playmates and I thought of her as a girl made out of sunlight and sky. I daydreamed about her and breathed her in and thought of her as all the superlatives—prettiest, smartest, best.

I don't know why that changed. I don't know *when* it changed. But you can't know Laurel without changing your opinion of her as she shape-shifts from one form to another before your eyes.

The girl you thought you knew will become one you don't recognize.

I've known her long enough now to understand that what lies beneath the facade is murky and dark. She is a bottomless pool in which it's dangerous to swim. You never know if something will pull you under.

So Laurel is my only experience of loving a girl, if whatever childish emotion I used to feel for her was love. It's not just that the village is too small a community, that everyone anywhere near my age feels like a sibling. Kids from the outside come to the village school, because it's known all over for its unconventional philosophy on education. So there are girls from the surrounding towns, some of them a world of possibility I can imagine on my brighter days.

But something holds me back from pursuing any of them. Even when they pursue me, I freeze up, my insides hard and cold, unable to enjoy the pleasures of flirting and being flirted with. Sooner or later, they give up.

Then I feel bad. I know I've probably missed out on something amazing, but it doesn't change anything. I am still frozen.

Laurel says I'm too aloof, too high-minded, too focused on the wrong things. But I know she's secretly glad I don't fall for any of the town girls. I can tell from the casual way she criticizes my aloofness, like she doesn't really care at all.

The new girl, though . . .

Nicole.

The dreams about her still plague me, when I'm asleep and when I'm awake.

I dream about her narrow arms and her easy stride through overgrown weeds. I wake up with her name on my lips and woven into the space between my every thought. How do I proceed on this new planet?

It's sometime in the early morning hours and I lie awake

in the new tree house, a mosquito buzzing at my ear. I swat it away for the third time and stare through the skylight at the stars above. I want, for once, not to be alone.

I imagine what it would be like to have Nicole lying here next to me, her warm, light-brown skin against mine, and electric impulses buzz through me. I get hard at that one simple thought.

Deep breaths as I both pull away from and move toward the feeling.

Desire.

I've felt it before, of course. Countless times. But not like this. Not tangled up in a crazy ache for one particular girl, who carries a gun and knows how to use it, who lives a life unfathomable to me, who knows nothing of my own strange world.

Maybe it's her contrast to me that's so appealing.

Most people from the village pair up with other people from the village eventually, once they realize that people from the outside just don't understand. The spiritual path they're on doesn't allow for detours into the secular world. But us kids of the spiritual seekers? It's not like we've chosen this world. Still, there's something so singular about it, we still choose other kids like us, maybe not from this village but definitely from among those who understand—those who've grown up in the counterculture, or what remains of it.

What would a girl like Nicole think of this world? What does she think of me?

I realize, in this lonely darkness, that for better or worse I have to find out.

. . .

Helene is my mother's oldest friend. They came to the village together when it was first getting started, and while my mom kept being an addict, Helene cleaned up her act, got a master's degree, and became the resident therapist at the village. She is sort of like a mother to me, if I thought of mothers as reliable people who give good advice.

I haven't talked to her since Annika came back, mostly because I know she will tell me how I have to give Annika another chance, and I have to forgive for my own sake, and it's all stuff I don't want to hear.

But she knows I've been avoiding her, so when I see a note stuck under my bedroom door, with my name scrawled in her handwriting across the front, my stomach sinks.

I pick it up and open the envelope. Inside is a piece of paper that says, "We need to talk. 3:00 today, my office. Love, Helene."

I drop it on my nightstand and turn away, thinking of reasons I can't meet her. I have chores. I have to work on the cabin. I want to see Nicole.

But it's 2:52 now. There is nothing I have to do that can't wait a half hour. As much as I don't want to hear what she has to say, I don't have it in me to blow her off, either.

I walk across the central courtyard and through the redwood grove to the main building. Inside, down at the end of the main hall, is Helene's office, a small room with large windows, handwoven Indian rugs, and potted ferns.

The door is standing slightly ajar, so I know she's not in session with anyone. When I knock, she calls for me to come in. The scent of incense hangs faintly in the air inside the room. Helene is sitting at her desk, her pen hovering over a notebook.

"My dear Wolf! What a treat!" she says, beaming at me as she stands up and rounds the desk to give me a hug.

Helene always smells citrusy. She is a thin but soft-bodied woman, sculpted by a lifetime of yoga postures into her current shape, strong but comfortable to hug. I get the sensation that she is shrinking on me, but it's just that I am getting so much taller than her lately.

"Are you busy?" I ask.

"Of course not. I'm glad you got my note. It's been too long." She motions for me to sit on the sofa that faces her desk, and she pulls up a cushioned chair so that she's sitting only a few feet away.

"When did you get back from Haiti?"

"My flight home was Sunday," she says.

Helene spends several months a year volunteering at an orphanage in one of the poorest parts of Haiti, and then she returns to the US and spends the rest of the year convincing rich people to donate money to the orphanage.

"How was the trip?"

"Devastating and beautiful, as always. You should go with me next time."

"Maybe I will," I say, then lean back into the couch, allowing the quiet and peace of the room to settle me. "I'm curious about that cryptic note you slipped under my door."

"I spent the day with Annika yesterday," she says by way of explanation.

"Right. She's back."

"And of course I immediately thought of you. How are you doing with it?"

I shrug. What is there to say, really? If anyone knows my complicated feelings about the situation, it's Helene.

"Have you spent much time with her?"

"No," I say.

"Is that your choice or hers?"

"Mine. She's been trying to reconnect." A tightness rises up in my throat and I force myself to breathe deeply.

I do not want a feelings-about-Mom therapy session. I glance at the door, wondering how difficult it will be to get away.

"It's part of her recovery process," Helene says.

"Yeah, making amends. She needs to check me off her list."

"I don't think she sees it that way."

I stare out the window beyond her desk, at an Australian fern the size of a tree, swaying in the breeze. It must have been planted before the all-native plant craze hit the village.

"Can I tell you what I think?"

A half smile creeps up on me. "You're going to, whether I want you to or not."

She laughs. "You know me too well."

I shrug. "I'm listening."

"I suspect you won't be able to find any kind of happiness until you make peace with Annika."

A laugh sort of dies in my mouth. "Make peace?"

She leans back in her chair and gives me a calculating look. "What would that look like for you?"

"I don't know."

"Think about it."

"I don't want to think about it."

"It's not like you to be so resistant," she says in her best calm-therapist voice.

"I don't want a therapy session."

"I'm sorry," Helene says. "I should have asked you."

"Maybe. But you knew I'd say no if you asked."

She smiles. "As smart as you are handsome."

We sit in silence for a few long moments.

"I don't believe her," I finally say, the words restless to get out of me now.

"About what?"

"About being sober. Staying sober."

She nods. "She has to earn back your trust."

I don't think it's possible, is what I want to say, but I don't. Instead, I just look at my dusty brown feet in a pair of old thongs. I have my mother's toes, squared off, each one a little shorter than the one before it. It's one of the few ways we are alike.

I have never drunk more than a beer, never touched a hard drug. I've smoked weed here and there, but never with any enthusiasm, and I stopped completely a few years ago in an effort to not be in any way like my mother.

"I didn't ask you here to put you on the spot, I promise."

"Then why?"

"I just wanted to talk as a friend." She leans forward as she says this, reaches out and places a hand on my forearm, grasping me as she gives me her "I'm serious" look.

"Then as a friend you'll understand why I'm not going to join the Annika fan club."

Her lips purse and she looks like she's going to say something, but then doesn't.

"Don't worry about me," I say.

"May I offer a bit of advice?"

"Sure."

"Now that your mother is back, let her succeed or fail without any help from you, okay? Just be open to the possibility of change, but know you don't have to control the outcome."

She has me there. I look into her faded blue eyes and know she sees my fear—of becoming stuck in my mother's quicksand-pit of a life again. She will suck me in until I drown.

"Okay," I say, and stand up to leave.

We hug, say our good-byes, and I go back down the hall to the front courtyard, where the afternoon sun is baking everything in sight.

*Let her succeed or fail on her own,* I think.

I can do that.

I can resist trying to save her from herself.

At least I hope I can.

This girl who has sprung up in my life like a weed—like a mysterious unknown flower—is a pleasant distraction from my mother. While I don't want any ties to this world, I also can't resist her pull. I have a plan of sorts, which doesn't include a girl named Nicole who hunts forest animals, but she seems to be making herself at home in my psyche nonetheless.

And she makes me wonder about the future. After the completion of the "tree house of Thoreaulike solitude" experience, after high school, then what? Will there be an escape?

A plan of some sort? It's only a year away and I can feel the restlessness growing in my limbs, the desire to get lost in the world far from here, to get away from everything that has defined me so far in life—my mother, the village, my father, my friends.

I am sure this earth has a million things to teach me that I can't learn here in the tiny world of the village.

In this way, I differ from my hero Thoreau. But then, his cabin in the woods didn't hover on the edge of a place that had threatened to swallow up his life.

Maybe part of Nicole's appeal for me is her otherworldliness, her stark contrast to everything I've ever known. She is from another planet than mine, and that must be why I come to her house bearing gifts.

Tokens of peace and goodwill, from my planet to hers.

If I don't extend a diplomatic hand, she might destroy me with her strange beauty.

I ride my bike along the gravel path and up the hill to the old farmhouse, and there is no one to be seen outside. The car and truck that arrived on the first day are still not anywhere to be seen, and for a moment I wonder if I should have waited until later in the day to come. But it's not so hot out yet, at nine in the morning. Later in the day would be a miserable trek. So I lean my bike against the side of the barn and walk along the path to the house.

What was once a brick walkway is now a patchwork of weeds and broken red brick. In the not-so-far distance, at the foot of the hill, I see a male turkey followed by three females wander into the clearing and I wonder if any of them will become this family's dinner.

My first instinct is to rush toward them and shoo them away to safety, but then, who am I to judge? A girl hunting her own food is far nobler than going to the store to buy a factory-farmed turkey, I know.

I have to keep reminding myself of this, because I am so disgusted by the sight of a gun.

I take the two muslin bags off the handlebars of my bike—one containing a handful of flowers gathered in the Sadhana garden by me just a little while ago, and one containing a loaf of rosemary bread baked early this morning by Laurel. This lapse of mine into neighborly hospitality is brought on by the sheer strangeness of having a neighbor, I tell myself. But a deeper voice reminds me that the neighbor is pretty—and ever present in my thoughts since her arrival.

Would I be bringing these peace offerings if it were only her dad who'd arrived, and not her?

Not a chance.

# Eight

NICOLE

About a week has passed since Dad left, and I am already sick of this little survival game. I wonder nearly every hour when he's going to come home. At least Izzy came back home last night, just before eleven, without any explanation of where she'd been or what she'd done.

I'm trying not to care.

I don't have the energy to worry about it, because everything about this house is falling apart.

But the big problem is still water. Or lack of it running through our pipes, as of last night.

We have plenty of drinking water stocked up in the garage, in gallon jugs lining the bottom shelves. I also know I can go down to the stream and get water to boil for use at home. And if all else fails, I have a supply of tablets for purifying water when it can't be boiled.

We aren't going to die or anything.

But after less than a day of no running water in the house, no easy way to water the garden, no easy way to take a bath, or cook, or flush the toilet, or wash my hands, I am starting to see just how spoiled we are in everyday life.

It's become a bizarrely lucky thing that our grandparents never bothered to get rid of the horrid little outhouse that sits in the backyard, because that's what we have to use now, spiders, bugs, awful smells, and all, until I sort out the water situation. Izzy and I got into a screaming argument about it at midnight last night, but once she understood how gross it would quickly become to have an unflushed toilet sitting in the house stewing in the heat, she gave in.

I've camped with Dad before, but I've never camped in my own house, and that's what this is starting to feel like.

I am sitting on the ground next to the well, its cap off, staring down into the darkness of it, when I hear footsteps on the dry grass. I look up, expecting to see Izzy coming toward me with yet another complaint, when I see Wolf instead, and my breath catches in my throat.

His presence is unsettling in ways I don't quite understand.

"Hi," he says, his eyes crinkling at the corners with a smile that doesn't reach his mouth.

He is carrying a couple of fabric bags, one with a bouquet of flowers poking out. For us? I almost laugh, because it's so far from what I need right now, which is a plumber.

"Hi."

"I come bearing welcome-to-the-neighborhood gifts,"

he says, holding up the bags and then setting them aside on the rear porch steps.

"Wow, thanks." He's like one of those military wives from the army post who used to show up bearing cookies in a country-style basket to welcome us to our new neighborhood.

"Did you lose something down there?" Kneeling next to me now, he peers into the hole.

"Not exactly. Our water in the house stopped working, and . . ." I think of the lie I've rehearsed in my head. "My parents went to the Bay Area for a couple of days to pick up some of our stuff we had in storage there."

"Hmm."

"Do you know anything about wells?"

"A little," he says, and my heart skips.

"There's definitely enough water in here," I say, picking up a flashlight and shining it down inside to show him. "I just don't know how to get to it."

He frowns like he's pondering the problem. Finally he says, "This house has been sitting vacant for so long, probably your pipes are rusted, and your starting to use them again caused one to burst."

"So we have to figure out where it broke?"

"You don't have any leaky spots in the house?"

"No."

"And you've tried all the faucets?"

"None work."

"Then I would think that might mean your break is between the house and the well, and it looks like it's an underground system. You'll probably need to dig to figure out where it is."

I look down at the ground below me. I am sitting on the space that needs to be dug out, and it's only a few feet, assuming the pipe goes straight from the closest side of the well to the closest point at the house, which is the kitchen wall where the sink is. This seems probable, and doable. Except the ground is hard as rock after months of no rain.

I sigh, not sure if I should reveal that I'm the one who will have to do the work. In a normal family, a normal situation, the teenage girl would, I guess, call her dad and tell him to come home and solve the problem. And then the dad would do that. Or he would call a plumber.

I don't want Wolf to know exactly how far from normal we are.

But he seems to guess my dilemma. "Want some help digging?"

I bite my lip and look up at him. "Really?"

"Sure, why not. Looks like you're on your own here otherwise. Do you have two shovels?"

"In the garage."

We stand up and head that way, and I wonder for the first time why Wolf is here. I've been so caught up in the water dilemma, I forgot to ask.

"I hear your little sister went hitchhiking last night," he says.

"What? How did you know?"

"She got picked up by my friends."

"Oh god. She's an idiot."

"She's lucky."

"Where did they take her?"

"Into town to a burger joint. They all ate together and then they dropped her back off here on their way home."

"Oh. She didn't mention. She's kind of a brat."

I open the garage door and blink while my eyes adjust to the change from bright to dark. On the nearest wall Dad has installed a series of hooks on which every shovel and garden implement imaginable hangs. I select a spade-shaped shovel, better for digging into hard earth, and hand it to Wolf. Then I grab a second one for myself.

"I don't know if your sister mentioned it, but we're having a party tonight at our place. You both are welcome to come."

"What kind of party?"

"Kind of a weird one, actually. My mom's throwing it to welcome herself back from rehab."

"Oh." I don't know what else to say, so I look at him to see how he feels about it.

"I have to warn you, my mother is nuts."

We are walking back toward the well, and I get the urge to tell him exactly how nuts my parents have been lately, too, but I don't.

"My friends said they already invited your little sister, so I wanted to make sure you got an invite too."

After my argument with Isabel last night, she vanished into her room and hasn't spoken to me since. I don't know what kind of response I was expecting to my acting like Dad, but I am sort of relieved not to have her making demands and complaining about every little thing.

I want to complain, too. I really do.

But who's going to listen or care?

"Thanks," I say, trying to imagine going off tonight to a party with a bunch of kids like Wolf.

I know without a doubt that I would not be allowed to go if our parents were here, and Izzy at fourteen would not in a million years be allowed to go. But a party . . . it's the sort of thing I sometimes fantasize about, wonder about, maybe even pine for, when I'm thinking about what it would be like to live in a normal family, to have normal rules, to be a normal teenager.

I have heard kids talk at school. I am not interested in getting drunk or using drugs or making out with guys in front of other people. But laughing and having fun? Acting stupid? Falling into swimming pools with my clothes on?

I am ashamed to admit it even to myself, but it sounds kind of great.

I want so badly to feel carefree, it takes my breath away when I allow myself to think about it.

"So does that mean you'll come?" Wolf says, a half smile on his lips.

We are back at the well, and I put my weight into trying to penetrate the ground with the tip of my shovel. I barely make a dent.

"I'm not sure."

All the true answers I can give sound completely lame. Like, that I'm not allowed to go to parties, that my sister is way too young, that my dad hates hippies and will kill us if he comes home and finds us off partying with a bunch of them.

"If it's lame, we'll just go do our own thing," he says. "I

can't guarantee you'll have a good time, but I can guarantee it'll be more fun than trying to dig up ruptured water pipes."

He grins, and I can't help but laugh. These past few days have been so completely ridiculous, I don't know what else to do.

"Good, it's settled then. You know how to get to the village?"

"No, I don't hang out in the woods watching people the way you do."

"You should. It can be illuminating."

"I bet."

"You just go down the hill and make a right on the next gravel road before you get to the main road. It's only about a half mile walk or bike ride, but if you want we could come get you in a friend's car."

"That's okay," I say. "We can walk. If we decide to go, I mean."

But the moment the words exit my mouth, I know we'll go. I can't really stop Isabel from going anyway, and I might as well be there to make sure she doesn't get into too much trouble.

Wolf motions me to step back, and I watch as he slams his shovel into the earth, penetrating far better than I could have managed. He has a decent hole dug in a matter of a few minutes, and I start working on making it deeper while he moves a foot closer to the house and continues to dig there.

My chest is tight with nerves, and I realize I don't feel at all like myself when he's around. I feel fuzzy headed, confused.

I'm going to have to be on my guard with him. He's got a certain wily, elusive quality that reminds me of real wolves in the wild.

We dig until we are drenched in sweat. The earth is so hard near the surface that it's slow going, but about a foot and a half down, the earth starts to get soft and wet, which has me exhilarated with the promise that maybe we've found the burst pipe. Wolf digs down another foot or so while I watch, being careful at the end not to dig his shovel too deep and hit pipe. Then we both get down on our knees and dig wet soil out with our hands. We are filthy by the time my hand hits metal, and I'm so hot I feel like I'm going to pass out, but I am grateful to Wolf for helping me. I wouldn't have figured out what to do without him, and I see that already all the preparation, all Dad's so-called training, didn't mean a thing when I faced an actual problem while trying to survive on my own.

I look over at Wolf, watching him as he unearths a rusted-out pipe with water spraying out, and I feel a surge of gratitude, and something else.

A buzzing, magnetic force, urging me to him.


## WOLF

I've never been a fan of parties, but the thought of Nicole coming to the one at Sadhana makes me feel like celebrating.

Maybe not celebrating the way Annika has in mind, with hand-holding and drums around the fire all night, but just feeling good . . . having fun.

I think I may have forgotten how to have fun.

I remember reading that Winston Churchill called depression "the black dog," and that is what I imagine has been following me around recently since my mother's return. Or maybe it's more of a storm cloud forever hovering overhead, turning all my thoughts and feelings gray. I never thought of myself as being depressed, but I realize as I ride my bike home from Nicole's house, my arms and legs and clothes stained with dirt, sweat soaked through my shirt, that I feel alive, really alive, for the first time in a while.

I want to know what happens next, which is not something I have been curious about for a long time.

We weren't able to fix her broken pipe problem. It's not like there were spare plumbing tools and pipe lying around. But she said she would call a plumber, and I was glad I could at least help a little. We ate some of the bread I brought over, and drank some water, and then I figured I'd better go, since I hadn't really been invited in the first place.

I jump into the pond when I get back to the village, let the cool water wash me clean, and then I spend the rest of the day avoiding the adults. They will ask me to do things—gather firewood, chop vegetables, set up tents for the overflow of out-of-town partiers who want to camp out tonight—and I just want to revel in this feeling of being happy for a while.

The rest of the pack, as I have my entire life thought of the kid group at the village, is scattered, some helping with party preparations, some doing their best to hide out and avoid any work.

I slip away to the tree house, where I spend the afternoon

nailing on the last of the roof tiles, and by the end of the day I am tired but exhilarated, my head buzzing with images of Nicole sweating, streaked with dirt, and working beside me.

She is even more of a mystery than I first thought when I saw her headed into the woods with the gun. She's a whole world unto herself, waiting to be explored.


## ISABEL

At first I thought the kids from the Sadhana place were weird. Like the homeless kids we saw on the sidewalk in Hollywood once when we went there to see the tourist stuff. But the more I talked to them, the more they seemed like the exact opposite of my sister and my dad, and therefore, the kind of people I can totally hang out with.

Plus that Kiva guy was kind of hot. And I think he liked me.

Then when they were driving me home last night and told me about the party, it felt like my life had finally started making some kind of sense. I almost cried I was so happy. Like seriously—tears of joy and all.

But then of course I returned to harsh reality, a house so disgusting I couldn't even let them drive me all the way up the hill to drop me off. I told them to stop halfway and I walked up. Seriously. I lied and said I didn't want anyone to see me catching a ride, that my family thought I'd gone for a hike in the woods.

And how to get ready for a party, with no running water? Oh my god. I had to stand in the tub and pour gallon jugs of water over myself. I'm not kidding. Nicole told me I could only use one but I used three, and I don't even care if we run out of water, because it's not my fault.

I'm going to the party smelling clean. That's all I care about.

# Nine

WOLF

I watch from my perch in an old tree house as people arrive
to the party. Most animals (including people) rarely look up,
so I can see everyone who comes and goes without them seeing me. I recognize most of the faces—people from town, a
few old-timers who used to live at the village back in its early
days, and plenty of my mom's cronies, her former party
crowd. This doesn't bode well for her staying sober. I've read
all the literature. I know she's supposed to avoid people she
used to party with, or else she'll slip back into old habits.

But like Helene said, I'm supposed to let her succeed or
fail on her own. Her staying sober is not my responsibility.

I can never tell with Annika what her true motives are.
She could be serious this time about wanting to stay sober,
or she could just be lying to herself.

I am starting to think Nicole won't show as I watch one
person after another pass by—all people I am not looking

for. I see Laurel return from town with Pauly, both of them carrying bags of ice for the party, and I am finally busted when they see me. They're the only ones who would think to look up to the tree house.

"Loser," Laurel says. "Come down here and help me carry this freaking ice."

"I'm busy," I say.

"Waiting for someone special?" says Pauly.

"Something like that."

"You're just trying to get out of doing any work," says Laurel, who knows me best.

"A little of both," I say, but now that my cover is blown, I might as well come down.

It's getting dark, and the scent of ganja is thick in the air. We carry the bags of ice to the coolers that line the patio and start dumping it in on top of the endless supply of beer. I feel my jaw tighten as I think of Annika here with all this temptation.

I don't have any control over what she does, but my problem has always been wanting to control it anyway.

Laurel grabs me by the arm and tries to pull me toward the sounds of music and voices behind the house, but I dig in my heels and refuse to be led.

"What?" she says.

"I'm not in the mood for noise."

"Ooh, big news there." She rolls her eyes. "Come on, please? I need someone to dance with."

"I'm sure you'll find plenty of dance partners."

Pauly swoops past us, catching Laurel as he passes. "I'll be your dance partner, babe."

She mouths, "Help me," but I just stand there and watch him whisk her away. There's no worry about him taking advantage of Laurel when she gets stoned or drunk, which is usually a problem. She likes to get taken advantage of.

She'd never call it that. But she's pretty, and wild, and willing to do anything for attention. It's a terrible combination. I used to try to protect her from herself, but I've learned over the years it's about as effective as trying to protect my mother from herself, or trying to stop anyone from doing anything they've got their mind set on, pretty much.

I am headed back out front to resume my post in the tree house when a heavy hand slaps the center of my back, good ol' boy style.

"Wolfgang, my man," a male voice says, and I turn to find Annika's new boyfriend beaming at me.

The smile doesn't reach his eyes.

"I was hoping we could have a talk, man to man."

"I'm a little busy," I say, edging toward the door.

"Nothing that can't wait, I'm sure. Let's take a sauna together, yeah?"

"Maybe later."

Or never. Never would be good.

He crosses his arms over his chest and frowns. "I'm starting to get the feeling you don't like me. Is that true?"

"I don't have any strong opinion of you one way or the other."

He flashes the false grin again. "I don't believe you. We might be family someday, so we need to work out whatever bad blood there is between us."

I hold up my hands as if this somehow makes clear my

lack of involvement in this whole family thing. "Whatever you've got going with Annika—"

"With your *mother,* you mean, also involves you."

"I'll be gone soon as I turn eighteen, which will be in a few months."

More like seven months, but still, I want him to fully understand the transient nature of my presence in his life.

I turn and head for the back door, pushing past a group of women I don't know, who've just wandered in.

When I'm outside again I blink as my eyes adjust to the darkness, and I am about to go back out front to the tree house when Nicole and her sister emerge from the darkness at the edge of the woods. Nicole is carrying a flashlight, and I'm instantly impressed that she dared to find a shortcut through the woods at this time of night, when the road would have been easier. It's the kind of thing I would do.

I wave my arm to get her attention as she surveys the scene, and her gaze settles on me. Her sister, beside her, is still scanning, probably looking for the guys she hitched a ride with. But she's a bit too young to be hanging with them on a night like this, when they will be up to no good.

I head over to them and am saying hi to Nicole when her sister makes a quick exit left.

Nicole, looking at me, doesn't notice until my gaze follows her sister.

"We might want to keep an eye on her," I say.

"I've had about enough of keeping an eye on her. She's determined to get away from me, so fine."

"You walked through the woods?"

"I found a trail when I was hunting and realized it led this way."

"You haven't been spying on me, have you?"

"I've been too busy with broken pipes and runaway sisters for that. Thank you again for your help today. It was really nice of you."

She looks me in the eye as she says this, and I can feel her gratitude. It makes me want to pull her close and bury my face in her hair, but instead I place a hand on her back and nudge her away from the house.

"How do you feel about tree houses at night?" I say.

"I don't know."

Although the one in front of the main house is the most useful for spying on incoming traffic, it was my first build, and the most utilitarian. It lacks the charm and funkiness that I like to think characterize my later work, and these are the ones I want to show her, so I lead her away from the main house to the western edge of the property.

From the back, we can hear a drum circle starting up. Out of sync at first, they slowly slip into a rhythm, and soon, if this party goes like the usual ones here, there will be a large group of partiers dancing to the beat, elaborately hula hooping, and generally letting loose. This is where things usually start to go downhill fast. I think of Nicole's little sister but decide to bite my tongue for now, since she doesn't seem in the mood to play chaperone. We will still have time later to catch up with her before things get too out of hand.

We climb the ladder into my favorite of the Sadhana tree houses, a circular one that sort of resembles a yurt. It has windows in the roof for looking up through the tree branches at the sky.

"Wow," she says. "You built this yourself?"

"I had a little help."

There's a futon mattress for us to sit on, and we watch people in the back dancing and milling around.

"This is all for your mom?" she asks.

"Yeah, pretty much. I mean, mostly it's an excuse to have a party, but people around here love Annika, so I guess they're happy to have her back."

"You don't sound like you are." I feel her eyes on me, and I glance over at her, then away again, unsure what to say.

Is it wrong to wish my mother had stayed away for good? Is that the kind of thing I can admit to a girl I barely know?

"It's complicated," I say.

"So what's your mother like?" Nicole asks me, and I try to think of the words.

*Wrecked, broken, unfathomable* come to mind, but I know that's not the whole truth.

She's also charismatic and magnetic and a lot of people can't resist her.

"She's an addict," I say. "Have you ever known an addict?"

I already know her answer to this question before she even shakes her head. Of course she hasn't. Her carefully planned and executed life thus far has only included the elements her father deemed appropriate, as far as I can tell.

I try to imagine a life growing up in the military, with an

army officer for a father, but it's so far from my reality, I can think only of stereotypes. And yet, Nicole is no stereotype.

"Does she use drugs?" she asks.

"Sometimes. And she drinks. Right now she's sober, but it never lasts for long."

"That sounds hard."

There is a strand of hair hanging down over her left eye, and I resist the urge to push it back away from her face. Maybe she wants it there, I think. Maybe it gives her a sense of hiding away. I know the need for that feeling.

I don't want to talk about Annika, though. This night is supposed to be fun, so I smile and shrug. "Hey, parents, what are you gonna do, right?"

She smiles. "Right."

"Have you ever been to a drum circle before?"

"No."

"Do you know how to hula hoop?"

She frowns. "Um, sort of?"

"Then let's go do some hula hooping," I say, and I start making my way down the ladder before she can protest. I know it's the one guaranteed way to get people to start relaxing at these village parties.

Near the bonfire we spot Nicole's sister laughing and dancing with the pack of kids I've grown up with, and I'm relieved at least to see she's not off in some dark corner pinned beneath some dude. I find two hula hoops, and there's already a group of people off to the side doing fancy hoop tricks, so we join the outer edges.

I look over at Nicole, and she's trying not to laugh. It's

one of those nicely awkward moments that almost never happens—the kind of moment where you know that right then and there, at least, everything is okay.

Better than okay. Everything is great.

## NICOLE

I try not to feel guilty about having attended my first real party, but it isn't until we make it home in the middle of the night and see that no one is there to catch us breaking the rules that I can totally relax. Izzy spent most of the night glued to a guy named Kiva, dancing too close to him, using moves I didn't even know she had. I never lost sight of her for more than a half hour, though, and she was in ridiculously good spirits when the party finally started winding down around two in the morning and I told her I wanted to go home.

She walked with me without complaint through the darkness, and this morning she woke up in a better mood than usual, even offering to help with chores.

I guess I'm in a better mood than usual too, though. I don't know what to think about Wolf and his strange life, but I know I can't resist liking him. I try to imagine what Dad would say if he saw Wolf come to take me out on a date, but it's too impossible to imagine. What if he just showed up as a friend, though? Dad would send him away, tell me I'm not allowed to associate with degenerates.

That's my best guess.

I get sick to my stomach when I think of those two worlds

colliding, and it makes me hope Dad doesn't come back any-time soon. Except, well, how long can we live here with no water, no air-conditioning, almost no money, no car. . . .

Not a lot longer.

I walk down the driveway to check the mail that I haven't remembered to check in a few days, and part of me wants to keep going all the way to Wolf's tree house and see if he's home. But I don't.

I open the old, rusted mailbox expecting to find bills, junk mail addressed to my grandfather, and those sales fly-ers that seem to arrive every day. But what is sitting at the very top of the stack is an envelope with familiar, careful, teacher handwriting in blue ink across the front. I take it out and study it, knowing in an instant that it's Mom's hand-writing.

There is no return address on the front, so I flip over the long white envelope and see there is none on that side either. There is only the letter addressed to me, and an American flag stamp, and the postal stamp of the date over the top, with "Barstow, CA," above the date on the stamp.

*Barstow?*

Why would she go back there?

It's the nearest town to the army post where we used to live. It's not a place she ever wanted to see again, as far as I know. But it's also a crossroads to other places—Las Vegas, Arizona, L.A., and south to Mexico.

I try to imagine where my mother might have been headed, but I can't. I try to picture her holed up in some seedy motel in the desert, and it seems about as likely as her running off to become a Las Vegas showgirl.

I realize I'm holding my breath, so I inhale and exhale slowly. Then repeat until my hands stop shaking.

I consider waiting to open the letter until I'm back at the house, out of this heat, but I am already tearing open the envelope because what if it's not a letter at all? What if it's something stupid like a recipe for Izzy's favorite pineapple cake?

I don't know why I think this is a possibility, but there it is.

Inside the envelope is a single lined sheet of paper folded in thirds. I take it out and can see blue-ink handwriting faintly through the paper. I open the letter and see the words "Dear Nicole and Isabel" at the top of the page.

Nearby, there is a fallen tree at the edge of the woods, shaded from the sun, so I go sit on it to read.

*I don't know if you will get this letter. Maybe your father will see it in the mail and keep it from you. I hope not. I want you both to know that I didn't mean to leave you behind. It's just that I know you'll be better off with your dad right now while I sort some things out. I guess what I need to make clear though, that maybe your dad hasn't told you yet, is I won't be coming back in any kind of permanent way. I would have rather told you in person, but I don't want to imagine you expecting one thing and then another thing happens. I will have to come get some of my things, perhaps, but I don't intend to live in that house.*

*It's not just the house though. Your father and I have problems bigger than that, and we are going to get a di-*

*vorce. I hope this isn't the first time you've heard about it or thought of it as a possibility. It won't be so bad though. Your dad loves you and will take good care of you, and both of you will be out of the house in a few years anyway. When I'm settled somewhere, I'll figure out when and where we can visit.*

*Until then, remember that I love you, and that this has nothing to do with either of you. It's between your dad and me.*

*Love,*

*Mom*

I stare at the letter, my eyes blurring. It's one short page, so matter-of-fact it's as if she's telling me about a trip to the grocery store. I mean, I guess I knew divorce was a possibility, but I never said it out loud in my head. I never really believed it would happen. I try to imagine just handing this letter over to Izzy, try to picture her reaction and how I will manage it.

She's going to flip. She might run away. And then I will have failed at the most important task Dad left me with. I can't even imagine Izzy taking care of herself on the street. She'd end up dead, or worse.

I carefully fold up the letter and put it back in the envelope. Stand up, dust myself off, and head back up the gravel road to the house, the weight in my stomach almost too heavy a load to carry.

*If Izzy sees this letter, what will happen?* is the only thing I can think. The bigger questions, about Mom and Dad, about the future of our family, I can't even consider right now.

# Ten

---

## NICOLE

I have always kept a journal, ever since I got one from a friend for my ninth birthday, though back then I called it a diary. It was purple and had the words "My Diary" on the cover, and it had one of those little gold locks with a tiny gold key that fit perfectly inside. I loved that gift more than any other I'd ever gotten, mostly because of the lock and key. I kept the key hidden in different places, trying to foil would-be snoopers, and I wrote in it every night until it was full and I had to use money I'd saved to buy another one, and another, and another.

I loved that I didn't have to write what my dad told me to in it. I could write anything I wanted. I could think anything I wanted. It was a dizzying sense of freedom.

It's funny, but looking back I know now that I saw even the lock as a symbol of freedom. It was what gave me the confidence to think and write whatever I wanted, without anyone reading it.

Without my dad reading it.

My first entries felt awkward, not knowing what was worth writing down, or what wasn't, not feeling confident that my own thoughts and feelings deserved to be recorded, but somewhere around the middle of that first diary, I started to find my groove. Our fourth-grade class went on a field trip to see a play about Helen Keller's life, and I remember being so exhilarated learning about her that I came home, went straight to my room, and glued my ticket stub from the performance to the next empty page in my diary. Then I did something I'd never done before. I started writing a letter to Helen Keller.

I wrote about what I'd learned from her, and it wasn't the last letter I wrote. After that, the letters came to me regularly. Letters to teachers, letters to friends, letters to the president, my parents, my sister, my grandparents I'd never met.

I wrote regular diary entries too, but the letters gave me a feeling I'd never had before. They made me feel powerful. In them, I could say anything I wanted to anyone at all, and any feeling I had pent up inside seemed to disappear into the pages of my diary. I felt light as air afterward.

So while I'm alone in the too-quiet house after the arrival of my mother's letter, I find an empty journal with a plain black cover in Dad's office, and I start writing.

But what comes out this time—it feels different. I realize it's because I'm literally writing to my dad this time. I'm writing something I want him to read, if he ever returns here. After all, what can he do to me, really, if he doesn't like what

I have to say? What can he do that's any worse than living in this broken-down house alone?

*August 3, 2002*

> By the time you return, maybe the end will have come.
> The End, as in the apocalypse, or the next ice age, or
> the Second Coming, or . . .

The longer our parents are gone, the more I start to wonder about them. Two weeks, and we haven't heard a word from Dad. I start to imagine the worst.

What I don't know about my parents could fill volumes of notebooks. I open the black journal and start with the questions I can think of:

> Where did Mom go?
> Why did she leave?
> Why didn't she take us?
> Why didn't she tell us she was leaving?
> Why did she feel like she had to sneak away?
> How did she meet Dad?
> Did she love him?
> Why did Dad retire from the army when he did?

Maybe these questions are connected, but I don't know how. I just know I want to find answers. I start by looking through my parents' stuff. Not just the obvious places, like the bottoms of drawers and backs of closets. I check those places, but I know I won't find anything there. I dig deeper, into boxes left unpacked in the garage, but my father isn't a saver of things that aren't useful. Mom, however, has a box somewhere, mementos. I remember coming across it once, years ago, but I haven't seen it recently. I wonder if she took it with her when she left. But Dad did all of her unpacking, so where would he have put it, or would he have thrown it away?

I turn away from my parents' closet to find Izzy standing in the doorway.

"What are you doing?" she says.

"Looking for something."

"You're snooping." She scans the room, taking in the open closet, the drawers I've failed to close all the way. "I'm telling Dad when he comes back."

I say nothing. If I act like I don't want our dad to find out, she's sure to tell him first chance she gets. Instead of arguing, I close the closet door and start putting everything else in the room back the way I found it.

Izzy gets bored and leaves, but I hear her call out in the hallway, "You'd better stay out of my stuff!"

I realize if there is anything to be found about Dad, it will probably be in the downstairs room he set up as his office. He keeps a locked file cabinet, but I don't know where the key is, and he has a laptop computer that he uses instead of the family computer, but he probably took it with him when he left.

For a moment I feel a pang of guilt for snooping. But then I think of the time that has passed with us here alone, no telephone, no way of contacting anyone, and the guilt fades.

This whole situation is crazy.

I doubt Dad has any important files on the desktop com-

puter we all use, so my best option for now is to try picking
the lock on the file cabinet. I can hear Izzy in her room,
listening to music now, so I creep past her door and through
the kitchen, where I stop to get a Leatherman tool out of the
utility drawer, then back to the office. I close the door behind
me and lock it, because I don't want Izzy to catch me trying
to break into the file cabinet.

It seems unlikely that Dad would keep anything all that
important in here. He has a fireproof metal box where he
keeps things like our birth certificates, a handgun, and I
don't know what else. He told me the handgun is there as a
last resort, in case all the other guns are stolen, and he said
he would give me the combination to the lockbox, but he
never did.

This file cabinet is an antique, something Dad inherited
from his own father, and it's made out of heavy oak, with a
lock that doesn't look too terribly strong. I open the Leatherman and pull out the tool tip that looks most likely to fit in
the keyhole. It doesn't fit. I check all the other implements,
but none of them are small enough, so I open a desk drawer
and rummage around until I find a paper clip.

I unfold the paper clip so that the end fits into the keyhole, and after some jiggling around, I feel a surge of victory
as the lock releases.

I roll out the top of three drawers and scan the headings
on the files, all neatly labeled in my father's careful handwriting and ordered alphabetically. I don't even know what I'm
looking for. The top drawer starts with "Auto" and goes
through "Homeowner Policy," with nothing in between
sounding all that promising.

Randomly, I pick up a file labeled "Firearms" and open it. Inside are some owner's manuals for guns, a few articles printed off the Internet about models of rifles, and the ownership certificates for all of Dad's weapons. He has most but not all of them registered.

I put the file back and close the drawer, then open the next one down, which starts with "Income Tax Docs" and goes through "Retirement." Every file has the sort of heading you'd expect a boring manila file to have, and I feel stupid for thinking I might easily uncover anything here that would tell me more about my parents' lives. I randomly pick out a file labeled "Household," because it's vague, and also because it's out of alphabetical order.

Placing it on my lap, I open it and find on top a receipt for a GE refrigerator. Next is an article about how to remove stains from carpet. I flip through and find more of the same. Exciting stuff.

After putting the file back, I open the bottom drawer and scan again for anything that might be helpful. The "Passports" file catches my eye, because I am pretty sure Dad keeps our passports in the locked fireproof box. When I open it, I find a photocopy of my parents' marriage certificate staring back at me. I pick it up and study it more closely. It has their full names and birth dates and says they were married at Fort Lewis, Washington, which is near where my mom went to college.

I do the math on their dates of birth and figure out for the first time my mom's age when she married Dad. She was twenty-one and he was thirty-four at the time—*thirteen years' difference?*

I try to imagine myself in five more years getting married to some thirty-four-year-old man and my stomach goes sour.

There is a photo I have seen of them as newlyweds, standing in front of a church, Mom wearing a simple white sundress and Dad wearing his army dress blues. They smile as if it hurts to do so. She looks impossibly young, like someone I could be friends with now.

I never used to wonder about their age difference. When I was young, I thought that was just how things went—Dad had some gray hairs and Mom didn't.

It also hasn't escaped my notice that no way in a million years would our dad let us date someone that much older, even if we were eighteen or nineteen. He'd flip out, I'm sure.

So why was it okay for him and Mom?

I'll have to add that to my list of questions in the journal.

I flip to the next paper after the marriage certificate copy, and I find a handwritten letter from my mom to my dad, on thick white linen paper with my mom's careful script in blue ink.

*Dear James,*

*I miss you, and I wonder what it's like for you in Bosnia. I know it's only been a month since your deployment, but I can't help wondering if I'm cut out for life as an army wife. It's a lonely life. If I'd known just how lonely, I'm not sure I would have gone dancing at the officers' club a year ago, or agreed to dance with you, or gave you my phone number after, or accepted your invitation to dinner.*

*I don't regret our meeting and falling in love, but I do wish I'd understood how hard it would be.*

*I try to be strong and keep my mind on my classroom, but something has come up that I need to let you know about. I'm pregnant, eight weeks along to be exact. I've been taking my birth control pills without fail, so I don't know how this happened. I wish I could tell you in person, or even over the phone, but every time we get a chance to talk, I just can't make the words come out.*

*What I need you to know is, while I understand you'd like to have children now, I'm not ready, and I don't know when or if I ever will be. I can't have a baby right now, not when I'm just getting on my feet as a teacher. This is the first year I feel like I know what I'm doing, and I'm excited about the progress I see in my students and in my own skills. I can't throw all that away now. I just can't.*

*This is almost as hard to write as it would be to say out loud. I have decided to end this pregnancy, I'm sorry to say. I sometimes think I should just do it without telling you, and you'd never know the difference, but in case something goes wrong, I want you to understand my reasons.*

*I hope you'll forgive me. I know when we talked before about having kids, you were sure I'd change my mind about not wanting to. You thought our love for each other would conquer my doubts. And I do love you—but I need you to love me enough to understand and accept my feelings. I trust that you do, and you will.*

*Love Always,*
*Maly*

Mom didn't want to have kids? I look at the date at the top of the page, and it's from five years before I was born. I let this sink in.

I might have had an older brother, or sister. I might never have been born at all. Maybe Mom changed her mind about having kids, or maybe Dad steamrolled over her wishes and insisted it happen. Though, from the sound of this letter, she would not have been easy to steamroll over.

The doorknob rattles, and then there is a knock. "Open up! What are you doing in there?" says Izzy from the other side of the door. I shove the papers back in the file cabinet, close it, and go to the door.

Before she can say anything, I push past her and run outside, down the stairs, across the yard, and toward the woods. I keep going until I'm far enough that I know she won't follow. Then I sit down on the ground and cry.

I never should have snooped around, if I couldn't handle the secrets I'd find. I understand that now, a day too late. So I lie awake, unable to sleep, trying to force my thoughts away from my mother and my father and their complicated history.

Whenever I hear the old REM song "It's the End of the World as We Know It (and I Feel Fine)," the lyrics get stuck in my head and won't leave me alone. When I was younger, I'd hear it come on the station my mom liked to listen to when we were in the car, and I'd think of Dad, always talking about how we had to get ready for the end of the world as we knew it, how only the smartest and most prepared would survive. I would think, why do the guys singing feel fine about the world as they knew it ending? Wasn't it scary?

Now the lyrics, forever burned into my memory through repetition, make perfect sense to me. The world as I know it isn't the kind of place I could ever feel safe in.

I lie in bed, listening to the sounds of rodents scratching around in the attic, and I feel as if the ceiling is going to come crashing down on me. It's so hot that I'm drenched in sweat, and the fan blowing hot air on me does nothing to cool me off, but I can't open the windows tonight because then we'll be breathing in acrid brown smoke from the forest fires burning in the hills nearby.

In one corner, bits of the ceiling are falling off, a semi-steady shower of white plaster crumbs forming a pile on the floor next to my bed. This sight, most of all, makes me want to scream, or break something, or do exactly what my mother did—run away from it all.

Except I can't run.

I'm trapped here with my bratty sister and no one to turn to for help. I could count on two hands the relatives we have ever met, people who might possibly be called for help in a normal family. But we are no normal family.

I barely know our distant cousins in Fresno, because no one in our family is all that close. My mom's family never liked my dad, and so we kept our distance. Maybe they would help if I called them, but I know deep down that I'm not ready to admit defeat.

I want to prove to myself—if not to Dad anymore—that I can handle this.

But *can* I handle it?

I don't have any choice.

# Eleven

WOLF

In the latter half of the 1800s people came here to this part of the country looking for gold. If you read about Gold Rush history, it's mostly about how people endured hardships, died, and fought to find their fortunes. I used to think they were all driven by greed. But then I realized how desperate some of those people had to be, to leave their homes, travel across country before there were cars or highways or planes or even many roads, and then struggle for years to find enough gold to survive on.

Maybe if I'd been alive then, I would have been a forty-niner too.

The older I get, the more I feel as if I am some lone explorer in a strange new world, where I understand few of the rules and am not sure I have the right equipment to survive. I think of Nicole and her hunting rifle, her finger poised so easily against the trigger, ready to take away any life she chose.

In this way, I can't escape Mahesh's teachings about peace and universal love, no matter how well I understand that we all have to survive however we know how.

There's a darkness that hovers at the edge of my thoughts. It's been there for as long as I can remember, and at least what I've learned from Mahesh helps me keep it at bay.

This darkness is what killed my father, according to my mom. Drove him to put a bullet in his head, a death so sudden and violent I cannot begin to fathom him inflicting it upon himself, my gentle, earth-loving father. That he would even touch a gun is incomprehensible to me, let alone aim at himself and pull the trigger. How would he even come to own an object capable of such destruction?

How could he destroy his own life so completely, leaving me behind with only his brown hair, his brown eyes, and his dark edges?

I'm glad I haven't seen Nicole with guns since that first day. I'm not sure I could call her a friend if she considered them her favorite objects.

I've invited her to see the Yuba River, which is an hour-and-a-half hike from the village but worth it if you set out early and bring water. Finding cold water to swim in seems like the only thing worth doing.

We walk along the path toward the river, gradually downhill, in silence for a short while.

She seems a bit subdued since the last time I saw her, a bit tired around the eyes, but she hasn't said if something is bothering her, and I don't ask. If she wants me to know, she'll tell me.

The sound of the rushing water can be heard now above

birds chirping overhead. The miracle of water, still here in spite of drought, always makes me grateful. It is frigid snow-melt, difficult to swim in and with treacherous currents in certain spots, but not here, where the arrangement of rocks and water creates a semiprotected pool, perfect for swimming.

When we enter the clearing, I hear Nicole exclaim something, and I turn to see her staring in awe.

"Wow. It's a real river."

"Yep. The great Yuba, as pretty as they come."

She smiles, and I know it was worth the long hike. She could have spent the day doing the endless list of chores her dad expects her to complete, but she's here with me instead.

"There used to be a lot more birds around," I say, feeling myself wanting to impress her with my skills of observation. "More animals of all kinds really, but the past few years, there are fewer and fewer."

"Why do you think?"

"Drought. Even the Yuba's a lot smaller than it used to be. I guess the wildlife have mostly died or migrated to spots with more water."

She stares at the dark woods across the river, seeming to give this some thought. "What's the best thing you've ever seen out here?"

*You* is what I almost say. Instead, I tell her about the next best thing. "I was out hiking once and got a little lost, so I ended up heading home in the dark. I was walking along a fire road when a young mountain lion ran across the road ahead, chasing a hare. The moon was out, and I could see them clearly, and I nearly pissed my pants."

Her expression goes from shocked to amused. "That's amazing. I'd have been terrified."

"He was only about fifty pounds or so, but yeah. I didn't go wandering around in the dark for a while after that."

I watch her move toward the water, then bend to touch it when she reaches the river's edge. I wonder if she's ever been kissed or touched.

I wonder if she would let me.

Or if I should even dare to hope.

It's not why I brought her here, or it's not consciously why, but as I watch her take off her shirt and shorts, revealing a one-piece blue swimsuit, I know that someday soon I want there to be more than a friendship between us.

I want to know her in ways I cannot fathom, and it's an urge so powerful, I feel as if the energy of all humanity past and present is pushing me toward it.

## NICOLE

What most people don't understand is that just because I know how to use a gun doesn't mean I like to do it.

But since the age of six, my dad has been trying to convert me. Mostly I have gone along with it. First it was just with an air rifle. He used to take me out in the backyard and have me aim at cans on the fence or homemade paper targets.

Once, though, when I was eight and had gotten so good at shooting targets and cans and tennis balls my dad threw into the air, he convinced me to aim at a squirrel, and when I actually hit it—when I watched its small brown body flinch and fall from the tree branch, landing with a quiet *thud* on the ground—I felt as if I'd just committed murder.

I *had* committed murder, as far as I was concerned then.

In that instant of realizing what an awful thing I'd done, I dropped the gun onto the ground and started to cry. My father tried to shush me, to tell me I'd done great, that the squirrel wasn't going to go to waste—heck, we could eat it for dinner, he'd said—but I was not comforted. I only cried harder, until my mother came out to see what was the matter, and I darted past her into the house and locked myself in my room for the rest of the night.

There, I'd huddled up under the covers, sobbing, torturing myself with images of starving baby squirrels in a nest somewhere, waiting for their mama or daddy squirrel to come back to them.

This was not an auspicious start to the hunting career my dad had hoped I would go on to have.

For years afterward, I had nightmares about the squirrel and its orphaned family. Always, in my dreams, I was happy to be firing the gun until the moment the squirrel hit the ground, and then I would be overcome with a guilt so intense it would freeze me to the spot, powerless as I watched the poor animal in its death throes. I would have the sense, too, that if I could only make myself move, to go to the squirrel and pick it up, take it inside and bandage it up, I could nurse it back to health. But I would wake up then, grieving all over again for my one and only kill.

After that, for years, I tried everything I could to get out of target practice, but my dad didn't give up easily on such things. Eventually I returned to gun practice, even graduating to a real rifle on my tenth birthday, and as I got older I began to understand that killing my own dinner was more humane than what happened to animals on factory farms, at least.

Becoming a vegetarian wasn't worth the fight in our household—not with my father the big hunter or my mother who had known starvation as a small child and didn't believe in being picky about food—so as long as I eat meat, I figure I should be okay with killing it. But I don't enjoy it, much to my father's disappointment.

Sometimes I think, for Dad, life has been nothing but one disappointment after another, me being the biggest disappointment of all.

There is the family he imagined (a whole football team-full of boys, complemented by a few dainty girls to help out Mom in the kitchen), and then there is the family he got (me and my uncooperative sister).

Now though, I don't care at all about disappointing my father. Our mother has vanished, and our father has gone off the deep end after her, and everything I thought I knew about them feels like a lie now, and the only way for us to get through this crazy summer is to stop worrying about their rules and make our own.

Izzy is slumped on the living room sofa, a fan two feet from her face and her bare feet propped on the coffee table in a way we'd never get away with if our parents were around.

I think about the stupid chore list, and how Dad said we would be getting the house ready for Mom, but she's clearly not coming back, and I'm finished doing backbreaking chores. Dad can do all of it when he comes back—*if* he comes back.

I go to the fridge and pour Izzy a glass of water. She looks like hell. I know she's been holding out the hope that Mom would come and rescue her from here, but with every day that passes, she seems more despondent, more aware of how unlikely any sort of rescue is now. We are pathetic, if this is how little it takes to do us in. In a real apocalypse, we'd be the first to die.

"Drink this," I say when I come back to the living room.

"Where were you?" she says, an accusation. "I've been stuck here all day bored out of my mind."

"I didn't realize you wanted me around for entertainment."

"I don't, dickweed. I just think if you're supposedly the one in charge, you shouldn't be running off with your weird boyfriend."

"He's not my boyfriend," I say and head for the kitchen, not wanting an argument.

"That's not what Mom and Dad will think when they come back. What if they get here when you're not home? You think I'm going to tell them you're just out gathering berries in the woods?"

I think of the letter I haven't showed Izzy yet. No way should I bring it up now, when she's already in a crappy mood. But it's so tempting to use it as a weapon, to hurt her with it.

"Whatever is going on with Mom's life now, it doesn't include us. Maybe she met a guy or something."

"Gross!"

"Well, maybe we don't really know her. Maybe she's having a midlife crisis or something. Maybe she's decided going

to graduate school is more interesting than raising a family."
I think of the second letter, the one in Dad's files about the
unwanted baby, and my stomach pitches. I try to imagine
showing it to Izzy too, but I can't. Not for her feelings so
much as my own. It's like if no one else knows about the letter, maybe it isn't really true.

I shrug. "It happens."

"Mom and Dad are *married*!" she says, and I clamp my
mouth shut tight.

She's talking like I would have before I knew about the
impending divorce, or the fact that Mom never wanted kids
in the first place.

If I can't protect myself from the worst of my parents' mis-
takes, maybe I can at least protect Izzy. I don't know how,
and I don't know why I even want to, but right now she's all
I have left for family. So maybe that's it. We have to stick
together, since no one else has stuck by us lately.

I sit down on the couch beside Izzy and put my feet up
too. I'm tired from the long hike, and I'm hungry, but I
don't want to spend another night eating beans for dinner.

"What if I take some of the money Dad left and we walk
to town and have a pizza or something?" I offer.

"Walk all the way to town?" She looks at me like I'm insane. "We could hitch a ride."

I bite my lip. It sounds like the exact opposite of what we
should be doing, but I don't want to be stuck here for another depressing night.

So I shrug. "Okay, why not."

Izzy looks at me doubtfully, but then a slow smile spreads
across her lips.

"Dad will freak if he finds out, you know," she says.

"I know. But he's not here, is he?"

She studies her newly painted hot pink fingernails. "Why do you think Dad was acting so crazy before he left?"

She asks me like she knows the answer and I don't. "Stress?" I say. "He doesn't quite know what to do with himself without the military."

"Do you really think he'll make us keep living here? Like forever?"

I do, but I don't want to say so right now.

"He just wants our life to feel like an adventure, I think."

Guys like our dad, they need to feel like the survival of the whole world rests on their shoulders. They need to feel like things are more meaningful than they really are. So they daydream about the coming apocalypse when they can act like heroes again, slaying bad guys and protecting their territory from marauders.

She sighs.

"Come on," I say. "Let's go hitch ourselves a ride to a pizza joint."

# Twelve

---

ISABEL

When I hear gravel crunching under tires, my stomach nearly jumps into my throat. I look up from the can of chicken noodle soup I'm heating over the stove at the window but can't see the driveway from here. I imagine Mom's car, or Dad's, or maybe . . . I don't even care who it is. I drop the wooden spoon into the pan and rush over to the window to stretch myself over the sink to see who's coming.

It's an old gray minivan that looks like something a homeless person would live in. I recognize it immediately as Pauly's.

"Nic!" I call out, stupidly.

I don't even know if she's in the house. I'm too excited to think straight, because no one fun has ever come here to the house before.

I remember to turn off the stove, super-responsible girl that I am, and I rush into the hall and yell for her again. But

I hear only silence in the house. Then I remember she said she was going out to the barn for something.

By the time I get to the front door I see that the van has stopped, and I feel giddy when Pauly climbs out the front passenger door. It's the whole group of kids from Sadhana Village, I can see now. Pauly and Kiva and Wolf and Laurel. I'm about to rush out the door when I realize I'm wearing a bleach-stained tank top and shorts from my morning of being a slave girl cleaning the house. And I must stink, thanks to no real showers in a while. I finally broke down and went down to the stupid creek to swim and wash off, but it was kind of disgusting washing in the same water the fish pee and poop in, and it's been a couple of days since then anyway.

Nicole comes out of the barn and walks up to their van, with her stupid hunter girl posture and her serious face, and I take that opportunity to hurry upstairs and try to clean myself up before I lose the chance to talk to normal humans.

Okay, no, those kids aren't normal, but they're better than my brainwashed sister anyway. A lot more fun.

Maybe they're here to invite us somewhere, which would be like the best thing that's happened since we moved to this horrible place, aside from the party they had.

In the bathroom I hurry to put on deodorant and smooth my hair back in a ponytail and brush my teeth and put on lip gloss.

Then I rush into my bedroom and grab a clean top and shorts and am still zipping and buttoning the shorts as I hurry back down the stairs. I've heard no more crunching gravel, so I know they're still here. At the front door I pause and take a deep breath and make like I'm just all casually coming out to see what's up.

All the kids are out of the van now. Laurel and the guy I don't know are leaning against it, and I'm struck by how impossibly cool Laurel always looks. It's not like I'd even want to wear the kind of weird clothes she wears—today it's some kind of white sarong thing—and I definitely wouldn't want my hair to be all tied up in scarves all the time, but she's so pretty and so different from every other girl I've ever seen, it's like she's this whole other species.

I used to hate my stick-straight hair, my boring brown eyes, my narrow boy hips. But then puberty hit, and everything about my body got curvy, and boys—even men—started noticing me, even staring at me, wherever I go. And I like it.

"Hey!" Pauly calls out when he sees me.

He is standing next to Nicole, who turns and frowns in my direction. She doesn't even have the sense to be happy we have visitors.

I smile and wave and try not to bounce over to them too fast. "What's up?" I say when I've crossed the yard.

"We came to see if you girls want to drive to the lake with us. We're going to swim and have a picnic."

I can already imagine Nicole's list of reasons we can't go, so I'm surprised when she doesn't immediately jump in and say no.

Instead, she just looks at me.

"That sounds cool," I say, then look back at her.

She shrugs. "Sure, we'll go."

I can hardly believe it.

First she hitches with me to town for pizza, and now this? It's the least irritating twenty-four hours I've ever experienced with her.

But then I see her look over at Wolf, the weirdest of all these kids, with his stillness and his silence—always like some kind of creature trying to blend into his surroundings—and I see something change in her face. I see, if I'm not going completely crazy from the heat, that she's got a thing for him.

I tuck this knowledge away for safekeeping, because I know it's going to come in handy. When I look over at Laurel, I see that she's watching Nicole too. Maybe she saw the same thing I saw. She's looking at Nicole in a weird way, like a hungry animal.

"Better get your swimsuits on," says Pauly.

"I'll be right back." I smile and go back inside to change.

I hear Nic following after me, but I'm in too good a mood to talk to her right now. I'm thinking instead about which swimsuit to wear. There's the one Dad approves of, a navy blue one-piece I wore to swim team last summer and that is all worn out in the butt from sitting on the edge of the pool, and then my black one, and then there's the new one he doesn't know about, which I bought with my own birthday money, the little yellow string bikini with the white beads at the ends of the strings. Of course I will wear it. I'm just a little worried about Nicole later telling Dad I wore it in front of guys.

But seriously? If there was ever a time and place for that bikini, this is it.

Unlike Nicole, I actually have a chest. Like a real, C-cup chest that guys notice. I put on the bikini with a pair of cut-off shorts and am walking past Nic's bedroom when she comes out wearing her own stupid swim team suit from last year. It makes her look like a ten-year-old girl, flat as a pancake.

"What?" she says when I grimace.

"Don't you have anything else?"

"No, what's wrong with this?"

I shrug. "Nothing."

She goes back in and puts on a tank top and shorts over it. Then I watch her worrying over her hair in the mirror, and I realize that I never see Nicole fixing her hair. Half the time she either braids it or puts it in a ponytail while walking to her next task, not even looking to see if she's done the job right. I seriously don't understand how she can care so little about her appearance.

Except now she does.

A few minutes later we all cram ourselves into the nasty old van. I am sitting in the backseat with Kiva, who, if I'm being completely honest, I will admit I have a little thing for. We kissed a tiny bit at the Sadhana party, and it was pretty awesome, but that was all. I haven't seen him much since then, and never alone.

The seats are stained and scratchy, and there's a smell like an old skunk. I search for a normal seatbelt, but there is just one of those lap-style ones, so I put it on and try to act like I'm cool with all of this. We are rolling through the woods to the main road when Kiva lights up a joint and takes a long hit on it, then offers it to me.

Okay, so I've never smoked anything before. Not even a cigarette. Someone offered me a hit at the party, but I waved it away like I saw another girl do, and no one seemed to care. This time feels different, more important. The smell is weird, but I don't want to start off looking like a dork before the fun has even gotten started. There's no denying that Kiva is cute, with wavy, dark-blond hair that hangs to his shoulders, and a dark tan, and pale blue eyes. He told me before that he's sixteen, so only two years older than me, definitely within reach.

So I take the joint and put it to my lips, trying to imitate what he did. Then I am coughing uncontrollably, my throat burning, my eyes watering.

Nicole looks over her shoulder at me with the same blank expression she wears when deciding whether she's going to shoot an animal.

## WOLF

I reach back and take the joint from Nicole's little sister while she's struggling to catch her breath. I put it out and stick it in the side door, because the last thing we need is to get pulled over with a van full of pot smoke, and also I'm sure our guests aren't big stoners.

"Hey, give it back," Kiva says.

"Not while we're driving, idiot."

"Okay, Grandma," he shoots back at me.

Kiva and I have never been all that close, but I've known him for as long as I can remember, and in that way he feels like a brother. He can be impulsive and dumb, but he's mostly harmless, and I don't want to see him in trouble.

I'm painfully aware of Nicole beside me, her brown legs smooth in the summer light, her thin arm close enough for me to brush against. Her hands, resting in her lap, are long and capable, with thin, squared-off fingers. Working hands, but attractive ones. I wonder if her palms are rough or soft, and I don't know which I'd hope for. Either would be perfect I think.

Up front Laurel and Pauly are arguing over the music on the radio, something about who the singer is, and I stare out the window at the passing landscape to wonder how I got here. I hadn't intended to spend the day with this group, but when Laurel said they were going to stop and invite Nicole and her sister along, I changed my mind. She could see straight through me, as if she knew I'd come along when she mentioned Nicole.

It's going to be over a hundred degrees today, so there isn't much else we can do besides swim. Even working on the cabin in the forest shade would be miserable, and I feel a lightness in my chest that I haven't felt in a long time. I'm glad to be here with my friends, on this sweltering day, hurtling toward possibilities. I feel young, or maybe youthful, instead of impossibly ancient.

We reach the lake and park along the side of the road to avoid paying the parking fee. It's a Thursday afternoon, but still there are quite a few people at the best-known beaches, so we grab our stuff and hike through the woods for a quarter mile to reach a hidden cove few people know about. It's partly shaded, a little beach barely emerging from the woods before plunging into cold, deep water, perfect for a day like this.

I carry the food basket, since I was responsible for packing it. Up ahead, Pauly has the cooler and everyone else has towels and blankets and backpacks. Nicole sticks close to me, and her silence is comfortable. I like that she doesn't try to make small talk while the rest of the group chatters away on the trail ahead of us.

There are lots of questions I want to ask her, but right now we're all hot and breathing hard from the uneven up- and downhill trail.

When we reach the beach, I'm happy we're the only ones there. We haven't even finished putting all the stuff down before Kiva has pulled off his shirt and jumped howling into the water. Nicole's little sister, looking precocious in a yellow bikini, follows him.

I get the glass bottle of kombucha out of Pauly's cooler and bring it to Nicole, who is spreading her towel out on the sand. She peers at it for a moment before taking it and drinking, then makes a face when she's done.

"That's not tea," she says.

"It's kombucha. Sorry, I should have mentioned. I've been making it all summer. Everyone at the village thinks it has healing powers."

"It's *what?*"

"It's a fermented drink made with this thing that's like a mushroom?"

She blinks, frowns.

"Don't worry, it's nothing dangerous. Just sort of a fizzy tea drink. There's water, too, if you want some."

I take a long drink myself and then offer the bottle back to her. She takes another drink, tentative at first.

"It takes some getting used to, I know."

She smiles then, barely. "It's not terrible."

Laurel has stripped down to a pale green crocheted bikini and stops beside us. "Coming in the water?"

"I will in a few," I say.

Nicole shrugs. "I think I'm going to check out those rocks first," she says, nodding at the opposite side of the cove, where rocks jut out of the water below a low cliff and a shallow cave.

"C'mon," I say. "I'll show you."

I'm eager to get away from Laurel and the wary look I can see in her eyes. Even though we've never dated, never been a couple, I know she still feels a little possessive of me. Like she doesn't want me but no one else is allowed to have me, either.

"Suit yourselves," she says, then turns and walks to the water's edge, where she pauses for a moment before jumping in.

Everyone is in the water by the time we make our way across the beach and over the rocky area to the cave. "When I was a kid and we came here, I used to pretend I was a caveman living in prehistoric times," I say.

"How far back does this go?" she asks as we peer into the darkness.

"Not far. I come here and camp every once in a while. It's so quiet out here at night."

Just then, Pauly yells and does a cannonball into the water, and the girls screech at getting splashed.

"Not quiet now," she says.

"When I heard you were invited, I figured I should come along to save you from the obnoxiousness."

"Do I look like I need saving?"

"No."

"What makes you think I would have even come along if you hadn't been with them?"

I look over at her then to see if she's serious, and she smiles, almost shyly, as if flirting is a thing she's never done before.

"I haven't seen your parents around," I say. "Will they mind you being gone when they get back?"

Her expression goes tense. "No, they won't mind."

"Are you sure?"

I don't want her dad getting pissed and not letting her come around us at all.

She sighs and sits down on the edge of the rocks near the water, her feet dangling. I sit down next to her.

"If I tell you something, can you keep it to yourself?"

"Sure."

She's quiet for long enough that I think maybe she's not going to tell me after all. I watch her as she stares out at the kids in the lake, and finally she speaks.

"My parents are gone, and I don't know when they're coming back. I'm not supposed to tell anyone, but . . ."

"But?"

"It's really hard. There's, like, no water in the house, and we're running out of food, and we have no easy way to get to the store, and I just hate not being able to talk about it to anyone."

"I thought you were going to call a plumber about the pipe."

She shakes her head. "Not enough money to pay one. I

sort of stopped the leak with a rag in a glass jar sealing off the pipe, and a bunch of duct tape holding it in place. But I have to re-do it every day."

"I can help. I mean, maybe I can fix the water problem, or else I'll know someone who can."

"No, I can't let anyone know we're there alone."

"We'll make something up to cover for you."

She sighs again. "I'm tired of lying to people, too."

"I can take you to the store. I can borrow someone's car, at least. Will that help?"

She looks at me, her brow furrowed, but she doesn't look as stressed out. "Yeah, thanks."

I wish we were here alone, so I could reach out and touch her. Maybe kiss her. Maybe more.

I definitely want to do more than kiss her. I've been thinking about it constantly since our swim in the Yuba River. Memories of her body, wet, glinting in the sun, moving so easily in the water, haunt me. I'm just not sure she'd ever want me to kiss her or touch her. And I mostly don't want to scare her away. I want to keep her near, so I can get to know her better, so this can comfortably become something more.

"Where did your parents go?"

"I don't know. My mom got mad and left, and my dad went to find her."

"So you don't know when he's coming back?"

She shakes her head, her expression one I can't read.

"Doesn't he call you or anything?"

"Telephones aren't really his thing."

"Too convenient?"

"Something like that." She picks up a stone and weighs it

in the palm of her hands. "He wants to see that we can survive without his help."

"Survive what?"

"Anything. Everything."

"Like, Armageddon?"

She smiles at this, but her expression is somehow grim too. "Maybe."

"Is your dad one of those survivalist types?"

"He prefers to be called a prepper."

"A what?"

"You know, like, preparing for the worst—prepping. I guess the survivalist label has gotten too much negative press or something."

"So that's why you hunt, and live in the middle of nowhere?"

"You live in the middle of nowhere, too."

"I live at a spiritual center my mother was one of the founding members of. They chose to buy land out here because it was beautiful and cheap and they thought it was conducive to spiritual reflection." I say all this without quite meaning to sound serious, but Nicole nods gravely, staring straight ahead.

"My dad's plan is to turn the property into a sort of off-the-grid fortress. He's even going to build a bunker."

"In case of nuclear war?"

"It could be used for any disaster."

"Do you believe in all that doomsday stuff?"

She shrugs. "We all have to die somehow, right?"

"For most of us it'll be when we're old, gray, and lying in bed."

"And the zombies climb through the window."

I laugh and look over at her to see if she's joking. She flashes a wry smile.

"So your dad has taught you how to survive in the wilderness? That's pretty useful, right?"

"Yeah. I mean, it is, but it's harder than I thought it would be. I feel pretty stupid with the house falling apart around me."

"That house was falling down long before you got there, so you don't have to take credit."

"Thanks. That makes me feel all better."

"I'm kind of handy with a hammer and nails, if you'd like some help doing repairs."

She glanced over at me, her expression wary. "Why would you want to help?"

"Why not?"

She says nothing to that.

"You know, I could use an extra pair of hands at my tree house for a few things, too. Maybe we could do a work trade."

"Maybe."

"How about I come over tomorrow and see what you're dealing with?"

She shrugs. "If you want to."

I look out at the lake, where the others are splashing each other, yelling and laughing, in some kind of boys-against-girls game. As if she can sense being watched, Laurel looks up at us then, and something about her expression shifts. Her mouth is still smiling, but her eyes aren't.

Nicole must have seen the same thing, because she asks, "Are you and Laurel, like, exes or something?"

"No. We're just friends," I say, unsure how to explain the whole relationship accurately.

"I get the feeling she doesn't like me."

"Yeah, I don't know. She's a little possessive of things that don't belong to her, if that makes any sense."

"So you've never, like, messed around with her or anything?"

"Oh god no. That would feel like messing around with my sister." I actually get a little nauseous at the thought, but I don't say so, for fear it'll make me sound like a freak.

Everyone is attracted to Laurel. She's like the mini version of my mother, only without the serious addictions.

"I know it doesn't make much sense," I continue. "But she's the same when it comes to my mother. It's like she wants my mom all to herself and gets annoyed whenever my mother wants to spend time with me."

"Wow."

"Like I said, it's complicated. She grew up without a family, so maybe since I'm the closest thing she has to a brother, she's afraid someone will steal me away? Same deal with her possessiveness over my mom."

"You feel like swimming yet?" she says.

I don't. I want to kiss her, to show her that Laurel's weird possessiveness doesn't make any difference, but I know it's not the right time, not the right setting.

So I take her hand. "Come on," I say. "Let's get wet."

# Thirteen

---

## WOLF

I show up the next day at the farmhouse, where it's still and quiet in the early morning. Only birdsong can be heard from the nearby trees. I've tried on the walk over to imagine what it must be like to live here alone, for two teenage girls. When no one was here, over the years, I've poked around this place, just curious. It was a nice house once, but it hasn't been cared for in decades.

I knock on the front door and wait. A minute later, Izzy opens the door and gazes sullenly at me. "What do you want?"

"I came to see Nicole. Is she around?"

"I don't know," she says, and closes the door in my face.

I wander around the side yard to the back and spot Nicole carrying a bucket of water across the field from the woods, so I go over and relieve her of it.

"Thanks," she says. "What are you doing here?"

"I said I'd come help out, remember?"

"Oh god, that's nice of you, but there's really nothing to be done other than maybe burn the place down and start over."

"Careful what you wish for," I say, nodding at the smoke on the horizon. The winds are blowing away from us again today, thankfully, so we don't have to breathe it in, but reminders of the summer fires are never far away.

"Hey, you know," I continue, "if you don't feel like sticking around here today, we could head over to my tree house and you could help me with a few things there. I need to sand the floors and a couple of other spots before I start painting."

"This was all just a way for you to get free labor, right?"

"Pretty much."

She smiles and shrugs. "Okay. It'll be nice to get away from here. My sister's in a mood."

As we walk through the woods she tells me about their hitchhiking trip to town for pizza.

"You should have let me know. I can always borrow my mom's car and give you a ride, you know."

"Thanks. I guess it was good at least this time to do something with Izzy, just the two of us. She's not handling things very well."

"So who picked you up on the road?"

"A nice family in a minivan. We got lucky, and I knew it, so I wasted twenty dollars for us to take a cab back home, since it was dark by then."

We reach the tree house and she stops to stare up at it.

"Here we are. Home sweet home," I say.

"I guess I was so surprised to see you here before, I didn't really notice how pretty this place is. I mean, it's weird but beautiful, you know?"

I smile. "You're the first person who's seen it, far as I know."

"Really?"

"I never intended to show anyone this place," I say.

She turns and gives me a look. "Why not?"

"I wanted to be alone."

"You want to live out here by yourself and never see anyone?"

"If I want to see someone, I'll go visit them."

"Oh, so you don't want visitors."

"No."

"Does that mean I can't come visit?"

"I showed you the place, right?"

"Not really. I found you here by accident, remember?" She crosses her arms over her chest and turns back to the tree house, regarding it as if it's a work of art in a museum.

"I brought you here today on purpose."

"For free labor."

"It's actually a labor trade," I counter. "But you can come visit any time," I say. "You're the one exception to my rule."

She smiles a little, and I realize how rare it is to see her smile. She has a face like calm water, rarely revealing what's happening beneath the surface.

I like that she doesn't have an easy smile, because I feel as if I'm witnessing something rare and beautiful when it happens.

"I'm honored."

"Can you keep my secret address a secret?"

"Of course."

She climbs up the ladder to the entrance, and I follow her inside. I didn't design this place to hold two people, didn't imagine another person ever entering and filling the space I don't occupy. The small room fills up with us, and I am aware of her closeness.

"What will you do out here all alone?" she asks as she peers out a window.

"Whatever I want."

Right now, what I want to do is kiss her, but when I lean a bit closer I can see her body tense, like a deer about to bolt. I wonder again if she has ever been kissed—really kissed.

"It's amazing," she says. "Like something out of a storybook."

"What is?"

"This tree house. Last time I was here, I was kind of distracted. I can't believe you've built it all yourself by hand. I'm impressed."

I suppose that was the point of bringing her here . . . to impress. But no. That's not what I want. I just wanted to show her a piece of myself that has nothing to do with the village or my mother or Laurel or anyone else.

I want someone to know who I am, separate from all that. I want Nicole to be that someone.

She looks away, then looks back at me, and I am surprised when she leans in this time and places a tentative kiss on my lips, like a question.

I feel only the fluttering softness of her, but then she lingers, and I pull her closer until she is pressed against me. I slide one hand up into her hair and cup the warm base of her head as the kiss deepens, and slowly we are melting into each other.

It's some kind of miracle, this kiss.

It goes on and on.

Every little molecule in my body wakes up, and the black fog lifts completely for the first time in recent memory. I am awake, fully here in this moment, alive.

Somehow, eventually, we stop kissing, and Nicole looks at me as if she is just as shocked as I am about this turn of events.

"Wow," she whispers.

"Yeah."

"We should do that again sometime."

"Soon," I say.

"Yeah, soon."

"Like right now."

And we do.


NICOLE


I'm no saint. I've thought about what it would be like to kiss a guy I like, to touch him, to lie pressed against someone.

I think about what it would be like to do all that with Wolf.

It keeps me awake at night.

But really kissing him is nothing like what I imagined.

I didn't realize it would be impossibly soft and hard at the same time. I couldn't have imagined how I would become electrified by it, dizzy and breathless and so lost in the moment that the rest of the world fades away. It's like nothing else I've ever known. You have to be in the middle of it to understand.

But then he stops and pulls away, and mumbles an apology.

"I really didn't bring you out here to make out," he says.

"I know."

"It's just I've wanted to do that for a while."

"I'm actually the one who kissed you," I point out.

He smiles. "Right. I forgot. I kissed you back, though."

"And then some."

"I don't want you to think I invited you into the woods alone just to perve on you."

"Maybe I'm the one perving on *you*."

He laughs. "You're the opposite of a pervert."

I shrug. "You haven't seen what I can do with sandpaper."

For the first time, our aloneness here feels illicit, and intoxicating.

I think of what my father would say, and then I push that knee-jerk habit away. It doesn't matter what he would say. What matters is what I want to do, and I want to be here with Wolf right now. I want to stop thinking like a little brainwashed girl and start thinking like I'm my own person with my own mind.

"This floor doesn't look like it needs sanding," I say, running my hand along the smooth surface.

"Not here, but over there." He nods at the other side of the little room.

I start to crawl across a green sleeping bag that's spread

out in the middle of the room, but halfway across I just sort of collapse, and there he is beside me.

"You don't really want to sand the floor, do you?" I say, as I pull him to me.

I don't know where this boldness has come from, but it's not anything my father has taught me.

## ISABEL

I'm not really sleeping, just lying in my room, half-awake, listening to the scratching sounds in the ceiling. Mice, I guess— or that's what Nic says the sounds are. But then there is this crashing sound in the kitchen and I bolt upright, my heart pounding in my ears. I try to get totally quiet so I can listen.

I've thought about break-ins, out here in the middle of nowhere, with no one to call for help except my dumb sister. And now I think it's really happening.

I scramble out of bed and tiptoe across the room when I hear no more noise downstairs. Then I peer out into the hallway, which is still and quiet. That's when I hear a scuffling sound downstairs. I run on silent feet into Nic's room and grab her shoulder.

"Nic!" I whisper as loud as I safely can.

"Mmm," she mumbles.

Somehow she is dead asleep while there is a rapist or a meth addict or a killer downstairs looking for us. I grab her arm and shake her.

"Nic! Wake up!"

Her eyes pop open, and she startles when she sees me so close.

"What?" she says, too loudly.

"Shh! There's someone downstairs!" I whisper.

She pushes herself up on her elbows, frowning in the moonlight that shines through the window.

"How do you know?"

"I heard noises."

"It must be Dad getting back," she says. "Or Mom."

"In the middle of the night? What if it's not them?"

She finally seems to register just how screwed we are, being here alone, and she sits up and reaches under the bed, where she now keeps her hunting rifle.

I watch her check the barrel for ammunition, and for once I'm relieved my sister is a weirdo gun nut like our dad.

Downstairs, there is only silence now, but I take this as a bad sign. Whoever is down there probably heard us up here and is now just waiting for us to come down so he can kill us.

Nic stands up and crosses the room to the door, and I hurry along behind her.

"What are you doing?"

"I'm going to see what the noise was."

Before I can stop her, she flicks on the stairway light. "Who's there?" she calls out, and I want to slap her.

Silence.

"Dad? Mom?"

Then there is a sort of scratching, shuffling sound, barely audible.

She takes a deep breath and exhales. "You stay here and

find a place to hide. If there's any trouble, go down the fire ladder in your room and run to Sadhana for help."

I look at her like she's lost her mind, but I can't think what to say. I don't remember when I've ever been so scared before.

"Stay here," I finally whisper, but she is already headed downstairs.

"Nic!" I call after her, and when she keeps going I edge closer to the hallway and peer down at her descending the stairs.

She vanishes around the corner of the staircase. A few seconds later I hear a gunshot and I nearly piss myself. Mouth dry, adrenaline pumping through my veins, I forget the safety plan and hurry down the stairs, unable to leave my sister alone down there.

What if Nicole is dead?

But she isn't. She's standing in the kitchen doorway, holding the gun barrel down. She turns and looks at me.

"Rats," she says. "Eating our food. I got one but the noise scared the others away."

I guess the sensation that fills me is relief, and then disgust when I peer into the kitchen to see a dead rat splattered against the tiles above the kitchen counter.

"Oh my god, I'm not cleaning that up."

She enters the kitchen and places the gun on the table before kneeling down to a dark hole below the cabinets. "This is how they're getting in," she says.

I think of all the scuffling sounds we've heard at night in the ceiling, and I imagine them being not cute little mice now but rats, like this fat gray one with its head blown off. It's nearly the size of a cat. Or was. The sight of it, and the scent of gunpowder in the air, makes me gag.

"What if there are more of them in here?"

"The other two ran back through this hole."

I cross my arms over my chest and scan the room and the hallway. I don't want to live in a house with rats so big it takes a rifle to scare them away.

"Why don't you check all the cabinets and the other rooms while I try to seal up this hole?"

I'm not going into the kitchen if there's any chance of a rat lurking, but I say nothing. I just watch as she heads to the front door and unlocks it, then takes the flashlight off the door-side table and turns it on.

"Where are you going?"

"To get some wood from the barn."

"Right now?"

"Would you rather I put out a little red carpet to welcome them in?"

"Screw you."

She goes outside and I am left standing here like an idiot. I can see a trail of rat turds across the kitchen floor. I've swept them up in the past, not thinking about what they might be. But now that I know what they came out of, I feel like I need to throw up.

My stomach gurgling, I find a pair of flip-flops to put on, and I search the kitchen and all the other rooms in the house. No sign of rats anywhere else, so I grab the broom and dustpan from the hall closet and sweep up all the turds I can find. Then I get the spray bottle of bleach water and start spraying down every surface. Nicole comes back in with a

hammer, nails, and a piece of wood, and she starts cover-
ing the hole.

I can't believe this is my stupid life now. While my friends
from school last year are vacationing in Hawaii, doing swim
team, hanging out at the beach, I'm scrubbing rat turd resi-
due off the kitchen floor in the middle of the night. Even if
I could talk to any of my friends now, I wouldn't want to. I'd
have to lie about every single thing that's happened to me this
summer.

There is a jumbo box of Cheerios that the rats have dragged
out of the cabinet and chewed a hole in the side of. Its con-
tents are spilling onto the counter now. I pick it up to throw
it away, but Nicole, standing up from having finished her
hole-patching job, stops me.

"We can still eat those," she says, because she's a lunatic.

"*You* can still eat them. I'm not eating anything with rat
saliva on it."

"The rats didn't lick every Cheerio that's still in the box.
We don't have that much food left."

I watch her open the junk drawer and repair the hole in
the box with a piece of silver duct tape.

"Oh my god. That's disgusting."

She ignores me and puts the box back into the cabinet.
On the floor there's a saltshaker that has rolled under the
kitchen table. Its falling from the counter must have been
the noise that woke me.

I go back to wiping down the counters, but I am so sick
of living this way I want to scream.

"This is child abuse," I say. "Maybe those guys at Sadhana
will let us live there until our parents come back."

"We're staying here. That's what Dad told us to do."

"He's not here! And he's not the perfect daddy you always act like he is, either," I blurt out.

I've never told Nic about the stuff I overheard our parents arguing about before we moved. I liked knowing something she didn't. But seriously, if she's going to let Dad ruin our lives, I want her to know what kind of asshole she's being so loyal to.

"What do you mean by that?"

I put down the cloth and the bottle of bleach spray and leave the room. I'm too mad to think straight, so I go upstairs and lie down with the lamp on next to my bed. It's still, like, a hundred degrees up here, even with the window open and the fan on, so I just lie there in the faintly smoky air and sweat, trying to think.

What do I tell her? What do I leave out? Is now really the right time?

I thought she'd gotten over her weird brainwashed state when it came to our dad. She's been acting so much cooler lately. But I guess when she gets freaked out or doesn't know what else to do she reverts to being Daddy's Little Robot.

I hear her footsteps on the stairs, and I brace myself for the talk where I set her straight about our father, but she doesn't come in. She just goes to her own room and closes the door hard behind her.

# Fourteen

---

NICOLE

Doing the laundry is a major ordeal with no running water to work the washing machine. I try to wear my clothes until they are really and truly dirty, and I try to make Izzy do the same. If she wants something washed before it's dirty, she has to do it herself is the rule.

So, before going down to the barely flowing creek to wash stuff, I sort through the clothes in the basket and take out anything that's still wearable. Then I go down early, before it gets too hot, and I scrub each piece of clothing or towel by hand in the cold water, using only a tiny bit of castile soap that's probably no good for the ecosystem, but when I tried doing it with no soap, everything started to stink too badly.

Then I bring them back up to the house to hang them on a line, where they dry stiff and scratchy.

When I get to the front of the house, Izzy is sitting in the shade on the front porch, a T-shirt wrapped around her head like a turban, bent over her toenails as she paints them scarlet red.

I haven't talked to her since the rat incident last night, and I can tell she's in a worse mood than usual, but I can't help it. She's being lazy while I'm scrubbing her dirty clothes. I drop the basket of wet laundry next to her.

"You need to hang these on the line before they start to mildew."

She doesn't bother to look up. "I'm busy."

"Your toenails can wait."

"Maybe I'll get to it when I'm done here."

I'm hungry, and my shirt is soaked through from sweating and washing clothes, and I don't want to fire up the stove to cook the endless supply of oatmeal we have. Nor do I want to eat the rat-tinged Cheerios any more than Izzy does. Not that I would ever tell her that.

I want to slap her, I'm so angry.

When I don't move, she finally looks up at me. "What?"

"Do it now. I have to make breakfast."

"I'm not eating anything from that rat-infested kitchen, so don't worry about cooking for me."

"You're being a spoiled brat."

Her face, so much like our mother's with its wide cheekbones and dark slashes for eyebrows, tightens with anger the same way Mom's does. Makes her look like a balloon about to burst.

"I'm not the spoiled brat—you are. You're the one who goes around acting like Dad appointed you to rule the universe."

I roll my eyes and turn to walk away.

To my back she says, "You have no idea what he's really like. You want to know the truth about Dad? He's a cheater, and a liar, and probably a criminal."

I blink. I can feel a drip of sweat trickling down the center of my back, and the feel of it is so infuriating I can hardly stand it.

"What are you talking about?" I spin around and ask as calmly as I can.

Izzy finishes putting a last stroke of red on her little toe, then caps the bottle. She looks at me carefully. "Dad didn't just retire from the army. He was *forced* to retire, because someone accused him of having an affair with one of his subordinate officers, and he could have been court-martialed."

"Just because someone says something happened—"

"It did happen. I know. It was true, and he only got to retire instead of going to trial because the JAG office didn't have enough proof."

"How do you know any of this?"

"It doesn't matter how I know."

"Then I don't believe you. You're just making it up to mess with me."

"Mom and Dad have been fighting over it for months, you idiot. If you didn't walk around with your head up Dad's ass, you might have noticed that our good old dad is a pervy creep."

I feel, suddenly, like all the blood has been drained out of me.

"I don't believe you," I say again. But really I don't believe myself.

"That's because you're an idiot. The only reason Mom was

willing to move up here was to get away from that whole scandal. And then she got here and saw what a dump this place is and she flipped out."

"Stop it! I don't want to hear your lies."

I have to get out of the heat and away from Izzy. I go up the stairs, past where she is sitting, and inside the front door, but she follows. And when I pour a glass of water from the jug in the fridge, I turn around to find her standing there, waiting for me to respond.

"Dad's not even here to defend himself," I say. "We shouldn't be talking about this. If it's true, then you can bring it up with him when he gets back."

"He's a liar, Nic! Don't you get it? He's not just going to admit everything he did wrong, because that's not part of the big lie he wants us to believe."

Tears are welling up in my eyes, but I refuse to cry in front of Izzy. I drink the water and put the glass beside the sink.

I want to believe my dad is not the kind of person she's describing. I want to believe he wouldn't lie to us and he's not a cheater. This is what I tell myself, but I'm starting to think Izzy is the only one here not lying to herself.

After all, what about the fact that he wanted kids and Mom didn't. Maybe that, and Mom's abortion, created a divide between them that never did heal. Maybe all kinds of things have gone on in their past that we don't know about, that we could never have imagined.

I think of the letter Mom sent that Izzy still hasn't seen. What Izzy is saying seems weirdly connected to it. Was this thing she's talking about the reason Mom wants a divorce?

I've kept the letter tucked into a cookbook that's sitting

on a shelf next to the refrigerator, so I go get it and bring it to her.

She looks at the envelope with Mom's handwriting.

"What is this?"

"A letter from Mom."

She gives me a suspicious look but opens it and starts reading. I can't guess what she's thinking by her blank expression as her gaze moves from line to line, but I know she has to be at least as upset by it as I was.

Before I can stop her, she crumples the letter in her hand and throws it across the room. I don't know why I think of going after it. I already know what it says, and it's not like some treasured keepsake I'm going to read again and again.

I stare at it stupidly, unable to think sensible thoughts. Some mean part of me wanted to hurt my sister, and I've succeeded. I know that much.

"Fuck you," she says, maybe to me, maybe to the letter, maybe to no one in particular, and leaves the house with a slammed door.

After she is gone, the old house seems to shudder in the silence, and I'm left alone with all my questions and doubts.

All the lectures Dad delivered to us over the years about honesty, all the preaching about honor and family and morality and right and wrong, and he cheated on Mom?

A wave of nausea hits me.

*It can't be true,* I think.

It can't be true.

Maybe he was framed, or the subordinate officer lied, or—

No.

I think about the past year or so and I can see how

everything changed. The tension between my parents growing, my dad's sudden retirement, his crazy idea to move us here to save us from Armageddon. It all makes sense when viewed with this additional piece of information. The puzzle takes shape, and it doesn't form a pretty picture.

Everything about my life that I thought was true is turning out to be a lie.

## ISABEL

I don't know where I thought I was going when I left the house. I just wanted to get the hell away.

I want that stupid house to just disappear. I want to hit fast-forward on my life until I'm as far as I can get away from here.

Mom not coming back makes no sense. That letter made no sense.

I trudge through the woods on the shortcut trail to Sadhana Village, anger burning through me. How could she leave me here? How could she ever think that would be okay?

I have the world's stupidest parents, and I'm completely finished giving a crap what either of them thinks or wants. I go to the door where I know Kiva lives, but he's not there. Some guy with a weird braided blond beard tells me I can find Kiva at the barn, so I head in the direction he points.

Kiva is hauling a bale of hay into the field next to the barn for some goats when I find him. The goats stink, but I guess they're kind of cute with their weird eyes and fat, round bellies. When he puts the hay down, one of the smaller goats immediately jumps on top of it and bleats.

"Hey," he says when he spots me.

I'm on the other side of the fence, but a little black and white goat comes over to check me out.

"Hey yourself. No pun intended."

"You've got great timing. I just finished my barn duties."

"Cool. You have time to hang out?"

He smiles. "Definitely. Come in here and I'll show you my secret hideaway."

I follow him through the open barn door. He climbs a ladder that goes up into a loft area, so I follow him. There, we're alone in the shadowy space, and it's all set up for lounging. A mattress, blankets, an electric fan, a radio. . . .

He crawls across the loft, flicks on the fan, and turns the radio on to some station that's playing what sounds like old-time rock. From behind the radio, Kiva pulls out a fat, clear bottle of something.

"Meet my friend Don Julio," he says. "He's here to help us celebrate the end of a hard day's work."

He takes the big, round cork out of the bottle and produces two shot glasses, then fills each with tequila.

I crawl over onto the edge of the mattress and get the exhilarated feeling that I'm finally entering a world I've chosen for myself, a world my parents can't touch, a world where I make all the rules.

When he offers me a shot glass, I know better than to

admit I've never really gotten drunk before—that I've never even tasted tequila. I just know it's what I want to do, so I drink it down fast, forcing myself not to react to the sharp, burning flavor.

When he sees the face I make involuntarily, Kiva smiles.

"It's good stuff, right?"

"Yeah," I lie.

He drinks his in one swallow and then pours us each another glass. Then another, when those are empty.

I am listening to him talk about a trip he took to Mexico, where he first tasted tequila, when a fuzzy blanket starts to descend over my thoughts and I feel a giddy sense of not caring what happens next.

When I try to tell him about how both of my parents are gone, that Nic and I are living alone—I don't know how many shots I've had—four?—my words seem to get stuck on my thick tongue, and I start to laugh.

"What did you say?" he says, laughing with me.

"My parents. They're gone," I finally get out.

"Gone where?"

"I don't know."

"For how long?"

I shrug, and my shoulders feel so loose they might go rolling across the floor. "A month maybe?"

"So you're on your own? That's cool."

I look at him and think about all the ways it could be cool that it's not. But I don't say anything. Instead, I scoot closer and lean forward until my lips are on his and we are kissing.

He smells like sweat and tastes like salt and tequila, and once we have started kissing we don't stop. Somehow we end up on the mattress, and he's on top of me, and this is the best I've ever felt in my life.

But at some point I realize there is no stopping what's happening. His hands are all over me, and clothes are coming off, and my thoughts move like molasses.

*I'm fourteen*, I manage to think. *I'm a virgin.*

Then our bare bodies, slippery with sweat, are pressed together, and I know there's something I should say about condoms or slowing down or birth control or I don't want to do this, but no words come out, because part of me does want to do this.

Part of me is on fire, and decisions aren't being made. There is this force pulling us along toward being closer and closer until he is pressed between my legs and I feel the sharp pain of his body pushing into mine.

No condom, nothing between us, and I cry out because it hurts way more than I thought it would. And it doesn't stop hurting as he keeps going, and somewhere on my lips is the word *stop*, but I don't think I ever really say it. Not out loud anyway.

He's up on his elbows and looking at me as he moves, and I feel as if I'm some task he's been given, a chore he has to complete, and there's no stopping until it's done.

Stupid tears drip down my face into my hair, but maybe it just looks like sweat, because he doesn't notice.

*I'm a virgin*, I should say.

No, I *was* a virgin. Not anymore.

He shudders and collapses on me, and then I am stuck there thinking about pregnancy and STDs and dying just because I was too stupid to mention condoms. To have one just in case. But who knew this was going to happen?

"Sorry," he says. "I meant to pull out. Guess I got a little carried away."

## NICOLE

I hear a car coming up the driveway, and I look to see headlights and the shape of Pauly's van in the near darkness. It stops out front and Izzy gets out of the passenger side and slams the door. The van pulls away.

She comes in looking awful, her hair a mess, her face pale and blotchy, her eyes squinty and weird. And she's not walking straight. She keeps listing one way and then another as she passes me and goes into the kitchen, where she flops into a chair and puts her head on the table.

I go in after her, pour a glass of water, set it beside her.

"Are you okay?" I can smell alcohol on her, so I'm guessing not.

"No," she says.

Izzy's story comes out in little bursts, not all at once. I'm surprised she's being so honest. Surprised she's willing to talk. She tells me about the barn, the drinking, then what came after.

"Did he force you?" I ask.

"No. I mean, I never told him to stop."

"But you were drunk."

I sit down at the table, put a hand on her arm, and she doesn't pull away. This isn't how I would want her first time to be.

She starts to cry.

"It's okay," I assure her. "You're going to be okay."

"He didn't use any protection," she says.

My stomach pitches, and I watch her face crumple like it did when she was a little girl. She still seems like a little girl to me, too young to deal with grown-up situations like this.

I hate my parents for making this a summer we're facing alone. I hate that I didn't protect Izzy, and I hate that I was the only one here to do it.

"We can go to a clinic and get you checked out, okay? And there's a pill you can take, you know, to make sure you aren't pregnant after the fact?"

I don't even know what I'm talking about, because this is not something I've ever dealt with. Is the morning-after pill even legal in California? I've heard about it, but I don't know. I've never needed to know.

"What if Mom and Dad find out?" she croaks.

"They're not here. How would they?"

She sniffles. "You're not going to tell them?"

"I guess if they want us to take care of ourselves, then how we do it is none of their business," I say slowly, only deciding it's true as the words form on my tongue.

After I've helped Izzy wash up with a gallon jug of water in the bathtub, after I've put her to bed, I stand alone in the living room, staring out the window into the darkness, feeling more alone than I've felt since we came here.

I've convinced my sister we're going to be okay. Or at least I think I have.

But will we?

I go to the bed and take my rifle out from under it. I run my hand along the cold barrel, cradling it close like a baby. Holding it calms me. You can't help but feel more powerful holding a gun. You can't help but feel like you can take care of yourself, if you know what to do with it. Maybe it's partly a delusion, but for once I am grateful for my dad's relentless focus on being prepared for disaster.

I wouldn't shoot a person unless I had to—unless there was no other choice—but I could fire warning shots. I could scare the hell out of some stupid boy who doesn't know a firearm from his own ass, if he ever dares to come near my sister again.

# PART THREE

# Survival, Evasion, Resistance, and Escape

*September 3*

Everything I thought I'd learned from Dad means something different than he intended. SERE was one of the first prepper acronyms he ever taught me: Survival, Evasion, Resistance, and Escape.

Survival, I know now, is the story you tell yourself to get by.

Evasion is all about avoiding the enemy. But what if the enemy is the person you're supposed to depend on? What if the enemy is inside your own head?

Resistance isn't a gun in hand, ready to fire. It's knowing your own mind. Knowing how you will bend, and how you won't.

Escape is not always physically possible, but no one can control where your thoughts go. No one can make you believe what you know is wrong.

# Fifteen

NICOLE

By the last week of August, wildfires are still burning in the bone-dry hills to the north, closer than any have been this summer, and a shift in wind could send them in our direction. Some people are voluntarily evacuating already, but with the river between the fire and us, I am sure we are safe. All we have is the radio for updates, and I keep it on until late at night, not sure what news I am listening for.

Izzy has been different since the incident in the barn, more subdued. I feel like a whole other person, too. I trust no one now, and it's as if this house is our rickety fortress against the world. I don't want to leave it, and neither does she. When I'm getting water, a sense of panic overtakes me, growing stronger the longer I'm away from the house and subsiding only when I've returned and locked the door. I sleep with the rifle under my pillow, hyperaware of every little sound, waking again and again throughout the night, more exhausted with each morning that passes.

I don't know what I'm waiting for, what danger I think is lurking. It's not as if Kiva has come around here, and even if he did, I don't really believe he's much of a threat.

It's something unnameable that I fear, some danger I sense lurking at the edge of the forest, some predatory force that knows our vulnerability and is waiting for the right moment to invade.

Izzy's period came two days after the thing with Kiva happened, and she hasn't wanted to go yet to the doctor for STD testing. I haven't had the energy to push her, nor have I wanted to hire a cab or to ask someone to drive us. It all just feels like too much to deal with.

I've asked her to stay away from the kids at Sadhana Village, and she surprises me by obeying. She worries me, even, because like me she barely wants to leave the house at all.

I am making beans and rice for dinner, for what must be the hundredth time this summer, when I hear a knock at the door. I know without looking that it's Wolf. He's the only person who doesn't drive to visit, and I never heard a car pull up.

I have avoided him since the incident with Izzy and Kiva. It's not like it was his fault, but I can't shake the feeling that what happened to her could have happened to me—maybe *should* have happened to me, if it was going to happen to anyone.

Maybe I wanted it. When we were making out in Wolf's tree house, I probably would have let him do anything, I thought at the time. But he was a gentleman. We only kissed, and kissed some more, and even lying there with him, he kept his hands in places that didn't threaten to get us carried away.

But now that it hasn't happened between us, I think it never will. Whatever I felt for Wolf is crowded out by fear for my sister's well-being. I understand now what it means to flirt with danger, and really I'm not a risk taker. I'm not the kind of person who chases thrills.

I turn off the stove burners and wipe my hands on a towel, my heart thudding at having to see Wolf now. When I open the door to him, he looks better than I remember.

"Hey," I say.

"Long time no see. Where've you been hiding?"

"Just here."

"I've stopped by a few times and knocked but didn't get an answer."

I shrug. I must have been out in the woods, and no way would Izzy have answered the door.

"Listen," I finally say, preparing for the excuse I've rehearsed in my head. "My dad's going to be back soon."

"He is?"

"I don't know when exactly, but he must be seeing the wildfires on the news. When he does come back, no way is he going to let me hang out with you, so we might as well just stop seeing each other now, before things get any more complicated."

Wolf's careful gaze makes me doubt my own words, but I don't waver. I just stare back, determined not to let him sway me. Inside, though, I feel like I'm dying.

"Does your dad have a thing about guys with long hair or something?"

I shrug. "Honestly, I'm just not allowed to see guys at all."

I know I've never sounded so lame in my life, but I figure it'll be hard for him to argue with the truth.

His expression doesn't change. He just nods. "I understand, living under his roof and all."

"Thanks," I say, relieved he doesn't argue.

He turns and starts to walk away, then stops and looks back at me. "Some rules really aren't worth following. If you ever want to say hi, you know where to find me."

I close the door, my chest hollow and tight, my heart thudding stupidly like a bird trapped in a too-small cage.

This is for the best, I know. It's the least complicated way to go, and mostly I'm relieved when he disappears down the driveway. But I also have a nagging sense that something has just gone horribly wrong.

## ISABEL

The night the wildfires jumped the Yuba River, we only found out later what had happened. We didn't think the fire could cross a river, and we didn't know about the overnight change in wind direction that sent the flames racing toward us rather than away.

## WOLF

The sounds of sirens and helicopters too close to the village wake me at dawn. Men's voices yelling commands are the next thing I register. The word *evacuate* enters my half-awake consciousness, and I open my eyes to look at the clock on my nightstand, but it is only a blank now. I attempt to switch on a lamp, but there's no light. Electricity must be out.

Fire, I realize. The odor of burning forest is more present now than ever.

I think of Nicole and her sister, with no car, no adults around, and now possibly no electricity. Who's going to tell them to evacuate? I sit up so fast my head spins, and I look around to see that my roommates, Kiva and Pauly, are a little slower to wake than I am. Probably sleeping off hangovers.

"Guys!" I shout. "Wake up!"

Kiva moans and rolls over. Pauly mutters something and pushes up on one elbow.

"What's going on?"

"I think we're evacuating for the wildfires."

"Shit," he says, and pushes himself out of bed.

Kiva's bed is on the other side of his, and Pauly grabs the blanket and pulls it off the sleeping lump. "Come on, man. Get your ass moving! We have to get out of here."

## NICOLE

I dream of someone pounding on the front door, and then I wake up and realize it's not a dream. There are other sounds, more distant—helicopters flying nearby, I think—and the acrid smell of the forest fires, as if it's just outside my bedroom window.

I jump out of bed and look to see what's going on. Pauly's

van is in the driveway, and I see Kiva standing next to it, looking up at the house. It's barely dawn, and my groggy brain can't put together why he would be here now, but a jolt of fear shoots through me.

"Open up!" calls whoever is pounding on the door. "Nicole! Izzy! It's Wolf! We have to evacuate!"

*The fire won't cross the river,* I think. *No way we are in immediate danger.* I know the evacuation is just a precaution, and I know I can't make Izzy get in a van with Kiva. No way.

So I grab the rifle from under my bed and I go to Izzy's room. She's already awake, just getting out of bed.

"What's going on?" she asks.

"The guys from Sadhana are out front. Something about evacuating for the fires."

"Kiva?" she asks.

I look at her and nod. "I'll tell them to leave. We can take care of ourselves."

"No!" she says. "Don't go down there. Please. Let's just stay here and wait for them to leave."

I try to think what the safest thing to do would be, but I can't. My dad's plan for fire has always been a well-stocked camper that we all get in and drive away. But he's not here, and neither is the camper. And I keep thinking, *No way could the fire cross the river.* That just makes no sense.

I peer through Izzy's curtains, careful not to show myself. Not answering the door is definitely the easier option. We have a fire escape ladder for her window, if for some reason they decided to . . . I don't know . . . break the door down? I can't imagine Wolf doing that, but if he thinks we're asleep during an evacuation, I don't know what he might do.

He stops pounding on the door and goes to the side of the house where we are now, looking up just as I duck out of the way. Then he starts yelling up at us. "Nicole! Izzy! Wake up!"

I hear what must be a small rock strike the house near the window. Then another. And then a third strikes the antique glass and comes through, landing near my feet.

Izzy looks at me with wide eyes, all her usual ironic attitude nowhere to be seen. She is sitting on the bed with her knees pulled to her chest, looking like a little girl.

Wolf and someone else—Pauly, I think—are calling for us outside still. Then there is some discussion between the two of them, Pauly wanting to leave and Wolf insisting they have to find us. Pauly points out that we may already be gone, and this silences Wolf.

After a while I hear someone try the back door, then bang on it hard. I'm doubly relieved one of the first things Dad did when we moved in was to install extra deadbolts on both of the doors and remind us to use them religiously. And I do. But a minute or two passes, and then I hear glass breaking, and my heart leaps in my chest as Izzy, still sitting on her bed, emits a whimper. I think of the utility room window, its proximity to the rear porch railing, how easy it would be to break the glass, unlatch it, and climb through.

I know in an instant this is what Wolf is doing, and with every fiber of my being I feel invaded.

"Nicole, you can't let them come in here!"

I look at Izzy, and her face is as pale as it was the day she came home from being with Kiva. She is a frightened kid, depending on me to keep her safe.

I know the rifle is loaded, and I cock it, causing a bullet to descend into the barrel.

"Don't worry," I say. "I won't." And I go down the stairs.

"Don't come in!" I call out as I near the bottom step, and just to make sure they know I'm serious, I fire a warning shot into the wall that faces the staircase.

The rifle blast is deafening in the small space, and the force of the shot slams the gun into my shoulder, but I barely feel it as I watch a cloud of dust from the lath and plaster wall settle below the large hole I've just blasted into it. I hear Wolf cursing from inside the house, and someone yells for him outside the house.

I lean against the stairwell wall, unable to face him if he is still downstairs. My hands shake, because this is the first time I've ever fired a gun to scare someone, and it feels more wrong than I thought it would.

It's only when I hear the van start up and drive away that I think to go to the back of the house to see how close the fires to the north look. From my parents' bedroom window, I see a black sky, a wall of smoke, so close the fire could be on our property. So close I don't know if we can even get out fast enough to escape it.

## WOLF

It feels wrong to leave Nicole in that house, but I've never been shot at before, and I don't even know what to think of someone who could aim a gun like that, and fire it, knowing a human being could be hurt or even killed. I don't know what she was thinking, or why she did it, but I got the message that she wanted me out.

It makes no sense, but then, little about her life does. I try to imagine how her warmth could shift to coldness, even violence, so quickly, and all I can think is that she regretted letting her guard down with me in the tree house. Regretted it in a big, big way apparently.

As we drive out to the main road I dial the fire department on Pauly's cell phone and give them Nicole's address, letting them know that two people in the house need to be evacuated.

## ISABEL

I guess I never thought much about the advantages of having a sister who's a gun nut. I mean, when I saw those guys get back in the van and pull away, I was so relieved I started crying like a freaking baby.

Then Nic came back into my room and told me we had to leave, and I was sure she'd lost her mind, until I saw the wall of black smoke above the hillside.

We gather what little we can in backpacks and run down the gravel driveway, the air heavy with smoke and ash, causing us to cough. My lungs and eyes burn. We've made it maybe halfway to the main road when we hear a fire truck's siren getting closer and closer, and then a red pickup truck with some kind of fire department logo on the side is upon us and we're being swept into it by strong hands.

As we bounce along in the truck on the main road, headed away from the fire, the last person I expect to see is our dad heading in the opposite direction—toward the house, in his truck. Nicole sees him at the same moment I do.

"That's our dad!" she calls out. "You have to stop him!"

## NICOLE

I watch through the truck window as my father is arrested for refusing to cooperate with the evacuation. His face, sunburned from wherever he has been, is also red from anger as he argues with the arresting officer who arrived on the scene soon after the fire truck we are riding in caught his attention and stopped him. He doesn't even seem to realize we are in the backseats of the truck, and I have no real desire to come face-to-face with him right now.

Aside from the fact that he will be humiliated at us seeing him in handcuffs, I'm filled with rage over everything, but especially that he left us to contend with so many things alone. Not the least of which is the fire that might be destroying everything we own, any minute now.

I feel some heat and pressure on my hand, and I look down to see Izzy's hand wrapped around mine. I don't know how long it's been like that, and I don't pull away, because I can't remember the last time she touched me voluntarily.

The police officer escorts my dad into the back of his car, then slams the door, and a moment later they are pulling away. It's only at the moment they are passing us that my dad's gaze finally meets mine through the police car window.

. . .

We find out the next day, after sleeping on a cot in an elementary school multipurpose room that had been set up as an evacuation center, that the fire didn't destroy our house. Firefighters were able to hold it off near the river and contain it, but we still won't be allowed to return to our property until the fire is fully under control. Our dad is released from jail after being held overnight, and he moves us to a motel room an hour away—the closest place he can find a room, he says, with so many people evacuated.

We don't bother to act happy to see him.

He doesn't bother to pretend he found Mom.

He is sunburned and silent, his shoulders slumped in a way I've never seen before.

"You've been watching the fire?" he asks me. I'm sitting at the foot of the bed I have to share with Izzy, staring at the TV news. Izzy is outside bonding with her cell phone, overjoyed to have a signal, finally.

"Yeah, well, listening on the radio for evacuation alerts."

It strikes me as ridiculous then that the one natural disaster we can't hunker down at home and stockpile for or protect ourselves against is fire. And that's the only natural disaster that might affect us anytime soon, far as I can tell. I wonder if Dad has thought of that, too.

"I saw the fires on the news and came back to make sure you two were safe."

"Where did you go?" I ask, not so much caring about his answer as needing to ask the question.

"I went down South. I didn't find your mother."

"She wrote us a letter that said she's filing for divorce."

He gave me a sharp look. "What?"

I shrug. "Is it true? About you having an affair with one of your junior officers?"

"No, and that's none of your damn business." He slams a hand onto the top of a nearby dresser and heads for the door.

I follow, because I know he's lying. I don't know how I know, but I do.

I just don't believe in him anymore.

"I know Mom never wanted to have kids, too. Is that why you cheated on her? For revenge, because she didn't want to keep churning out babies for you?"

Izzy opens the motel room door just then and hovers there in the light.

He turns on me, all six foot two inches of him, and his palm strikes my cheek before I even see it coming. The force of it knocks my head sideways. I stagger and then regain my footing, staring at him without flinching. I remember the opposite scene playing out between Mom and Dad, and I almost laugh that we have somehow become the family that slaps each other.

I dare him with my stinging eyes to do it again. Izzy looks nervously from me to him and back again.

My cheek is on fire, probably bright red with the imprint of his hand.

"She was right to leave you," I say, even if I don't totally believe it.

I just want to hurt him, or see if I can. I think he's going to hit me again, but instead he turns and walks into the bathroom, slamming the door behind him.

When I look over for Izzy, she's not in the doorway anymore. She's not anywhere to be seen.

## LAUREL

Everyone is able to return to the village four days after the evacuation. The winds have shifted and the Oasis Ridge fire, the one closest to us, is considered totally contained. I try to imagine where I would go if the village burned down, but I can't. I know for sure now that I don't want to find my parents, and I don't feel ready to be on my own.

When I see Annika struggling to carry a large box across the courtyard, I call after her and run to catch up.

"Need some help with that?" I ask.

"Could you just get the door to the general store for me?" she asks, and I hurry ahead to open it for her.

"Mailing someone a present?"

"Actually I'm mailing some of my things to Berlin," she says as she eases past me into the store.

I want to ask why, but she is busy talking to the store clerk now, asking for a customs form. I wait while she fills it out and completes the mailing, and then I follow her back outside.

"I've been meaning to talk to you," she says when we are alone again.

My stupid heart leaps a little. "Oh?"

"I'm thinking that maybe the fire coming so close was a sign, you know? It's like my addiction. If I'm not careful, I'll destroy everything."

"But you are being careful, right? You're sober."

She slips one arm around my waist, pulling me along beside her as she walks. "I'm sober, barely. It's just hard here, you know? So many temptations, old habits, old friends. I don't know if I can keep it up, and I've been praying about what to do."

The praying again.

"Okay?"

"I think the fire was God's answer to my prayers. I think he's telling me I should go, if I want to save myself."

"Go where?"

"Anywhere, but I've always wanted to live in Berlin, so I will go there, I think."

I don't know what to say to this. I'm stunned. I can't imagine Sadhana permanently without Annika. It's like the sky being permanently without the sun. It would make no sense.

"But—"

"I wanted to tell you first," she says, "Because I am afraid of how Wolf will take the news. He's going to need the support of his friends."

"Yeah," I say, not really listening, because I'm thinking, *But what about me?*

"Have you thought of taking him with you?" I ask, when really what I wanted to say was that I want to go with her.

"I'm going to offer that, yes," she says. "I just don't think he will like that idea."

"He might," I say halfheartedly.

"I've talked to Helene about all of this, and I know she thinks I ought to stay here at least until Wolf graduates, but I just don't know if I can."

"Helene knows what she's talking about," I say. "Maybe you should listen to her."

She stops walking and turns to give me a hug. "You're very dear to me, you know. Like a daughter."

I melt into the hug, tears burning my eyes. I want to say so many things. I want to cling to her and tell her she is the world to me, but instead I just close my eyes and inhale her scent, which is a mix of lavender and beeswax soap.

"I'll go with you if he doesn't," I finally say.

"But what about your plans?" she says. "I want you to make some, you know."

And I listen as she offers me real, momlike advice.

I go back to my room, relieved that no roommates are there, and lie on my bed, too shocked to cry, too sad to move. I think about Annika leaving, and her advice, and I feel a strange sense that I will do exactly what she's told me to do. I don't know how long I've been lying there when I hear a knock at the door, and I open it to find Isabel.

She wants to know if I can give her a ride into town. I don't ask why. I have already decided I am going there to register for classes at the junior college in the fall, and I hate the thought of going alone for this particularly depressing task. I keep thinking some better chance will come along, but for now I will do what Annika has told me to do. Sign up for college, plan for the future, be practical. It's the last advice I expected to get from her.

Izzy is carrying a duffel bag as she follows me out to my car and climbs into the passenger seat.

"What's up with the bag?" I ask.

"Oh, nothing. Just some stuff."

I know this isn't anywhere near the truth, but I let it go and drive through the Sadhana entrance and on to the main road. She straightens her hair in the visor mirror.

"Where am I dropping you off?" I ask when she says nothing.

"Just in town, wherever."

"Are you, like, running away or something?"

I glance over and catch a guilty look cross her face.

"You don't know what it's like at my house. My dad is insane. I can't stay there."

"So you're headed where?"

"To L.A. I know I can get a modeling job or something. I've got money saved up."

"That's the stupidest plan I've ever heard," I say as I pull the car over to the side of the road.

I don't know why I even care about what this dumb girl does or doesn't do. Maybe she reminds me of myself a little.

When I start making a U-turn to go back the other way she screeches, "What are you doing?"

"I'm taking you to Sadhana, so just chill out."

"I don't want to go there, okay? Just let me back out and I'll get another ride."

"You're going to hitch a ride all the way to L.A.?"

"No, just to the Greyhound bus station."

"I want you to talk to someone before you do anything."

"Not Kiva. I don't want to see him."

"Of course not Kiva."

"You're not going to talk me out of this, you know." Her arms crossed over her chest, she's glaring out the front window.

"No, I'm not. But you need some good advice, and I don't have any to give."

Five minutes later I'm walking her to Helene's cabin, located on the quietest end of the village. She's the only person I know who can talk sense into a dumb teenager, even if she has never been able to talk any sense into me. She's gained a new respect from me for trying to convince Annika to stay here. I knock on Helene's door, and when she answers I explain the situation. Izzy looks at me like she wants to kill me.

But one benevolent smile from Helene, and a few kind words, and I know she'll chill out.

"I've got to go," I say, and I leave Izzy there, in more responsible hands than mine.

Now that I've done my good deed, my first responsible adult act, I wonder what's next. College? A job? A pension plan? Two-point-five kids and a husband?

Maybe not, but I am starting to not feel so hopeless about the idea of taking one little step forward and seeing what happens.

I am not the girl the world sees. I'm not what everyone thinks I am.

I don't even know who I am anymore, but maybe I'm ready to find out.

As I head back toward the car I watch Annika stride down the gravel path, away from me, her skirt flowing around her calves, the late afternoon sun glistening on her hair, and I feel an ache in my chest that I know now will never quite go away. Or maybe it will someday when I'm not paying attention.

Then I get in my car and drive off to register for classes.

# Sixteen

ISABEL

With Mom gone and Dad acting like the end of the world finally arrived and he was totally unprepared, Nicole and I were able to convince him of one thing. He is letting us go to the high school in town. That might not sound like much of a victory, but try being in our house 24/7 and see if you wouldn't like to hop on a yellow school bus and head off to a typical American school.

Really he agreed to this only because he had no interest in homeschooling us himself. That kind of thing is women's work, according to Dad.

Whatever.

I am a freshman walking through the crowded, noisy halls, feeling like I'm a star in my own high school movie. It's just like I pictured it would be, way better than middle school. I scan the numbers on the doors, trying to find my first-period class, and when I do, there is a cute guy sitting in the first row. He looks up at me and I look away.

I have promised myself no more guys, not anytime soon. I don't know what to do with all the feelings about what happened with Kiva, but I know I need time, and I know I need to not be so stupid again. I think of that woman Helene, who I've gone back and talked to a couple of times now. She's offered to be my therapist or whatever for free, and I like talking to her.

Nicole was less interested than I was in attending the high school, but she didn't put up a fight. She rode the bus in silence with me this morning, probably as relieved as I was to be getting away from Dad.

In the time he's been back he's been working like a lunatic to fix all the things that are wrong with the house. It's a long list, so it's hard to tell he's done much.

He doesn't talk about Mom, but we got another letter from her a few days ago, explaining that she's enrolled in graduate school at UC Davis, only a few hours away. She said she's volunteering at the MIND Institute and hoping to get hired there sometime. She's learning something called applied behavior analysis, and she actually sounded pretty happy and excited about the whole thing, working with screwed-up kids and all. I don't get the appeal, but whatever. I guess it's cool that she's happy, and she said she'll be able to visit us soon and have us down for weekends whenever she can afford to get a place of her own.

Dad also doesn't seem to notice that Nicole has stopped obeying his every order. Since the day he hit her, she hasn't really spoken to him much at all, except for the bare minimum.

I like her a lot better this way, the new, defiant Nicole. She's the kind of person I don't mind being sisters with, especially since she blew a hole in the wall just to scare off Kiva and those other guys for me. She's the kind of sister I could maybe even be a little bit proud of, if she ever put on cuter clothes.

## WOLF

Annika finds me in the chicken run, communing with the hens, who search for bugs and pluck at the rare green sprout emerging from the earth. They have lost interest in me now that they've gone through the bits of sandwich left over from my lunch, and I can watch them in their silly gracelessness. She is driving past when she sees me sitting there amid a trio of Barred Rocks, beautiful birds with black and white fringed feathers. Her car edges to the side of the dirt road, and my stomach sinks when she kills the engine.

She comes striding toward me with purpose, a white skirt flowing around her legs, her hair pulled back in a bun. Thanks to a pair of sunglasses, I have no sense of whether this visit will be a hassle.

"Wolfie," she calls. "I've been hoping to find you, and here you are among the chickens."

To this I say nothing, just watch as she opens the gate and lifts the hem of her skirt to cross the yard. A few moments later she sits down next to me on the grass and sighs.

"It seems like you've been hiding from me," she says.

"Not really."

"School starts back tomorrow, yes?"

I shrug. My transition year, which is what senior year is called at the World Peace School. Transition to adulthood, for whatever it's worth. I can't imagine how it matters now, after this summer of strangeness.

"Aren't you going?"

"I don't know."

"Maybe it would be good to have a change of scenery. I've been thinking of going back to Germany. Would you care to join me?"

This surprises me so much I don't know what to say. Annika has never expressed any real desire to return to her home country. She's about as American as any German can get, far as I can tell.

I wonder about the boyfriend, whether he will be going, but I don't dare ask.

"Why?" I finally croak, my throat oddly constricted.

"Why am I thinking of going or why am I asking you to come?"

"Both."

"I met someone while I was in rehab. He's invited me to come live in his flat in Berlin."

"You met someone who isn't Mark, in rehab?"

"Mark and I aren't working out so well. He understands."

"So you're asking me if I want to come live with you and some guy I don't know in Berlin."

"You could visit and decide for yourself if you want to stay or come back here."

"No," I say, without giving it another thought.

Another deep sigh. For a while she says nothing, and the boldest of the flock of chickens, Lulu, comes close and pecks at my foot.

"The thing is, this is not an easy place for me to stay sober. I think Berlin will be better, with my friend who's also sober."

"Good for you."

"I don't think I should go without you. I'm still your mother, you know."

"That's debatable," I say, knee-jerk, without considering my own cruelty until the words have left my mouth.

"You have every right to be angry."

"Great."

"What I'm saying is, I want to go, but I won't go without you."

"You're going to force me to go to Germany?"

She is silent again, her gaze drifting from me to the horizon and back again.

"I won't go if you don't want to come. I'll stay here."

"Please don't. Not on account of me. I'll be fine here on my own."

"I left you for a year, Wolf, and I came back to find you anything but fine."

I start to stand up, unwilling to hear an amateur analysis of my psychic state, but her firm grasp on my arm stops me short.

"We're not finished here," she says, in her rarely used Mom voice.

I slump back down, crossing my arms over my knees and staring straight ahead to avoid any meaningful eye contact.

"You can't close yourself off from the world. It's not healthy. It's what your father did."

This parallel between myself and my dad is not what I want to hear right now. "There's a big difference. He numbed himself with drugs. I don't."

"I'm glad you don't. You're a stronger person than he was, and a stronger person than I am. I'm proud of you, you know."

I cringe, but something occurs to me. What if she's really going to stay sober this time?

What if she means what she says?

When I look over at Annika I see the same woman I've always known. I have survived a life with her by trying to protect her from herself, trying to protect myself from her, not really accomplishing either.

"I know it's hard to trust an addict, Wolf. I know I've never given you much reason to trust me, so you're smart to be wary. But I'm not going to leave you again."

She says this last part as if she's only just decided in that moment that it's true. And I don't know—maybe that's good enough for a start.

"Suit yourself," I say, my throat so tight words can barely fit through.

She puts an arm around my shoulder, and this time I don't pull away.


When the oppressive heat of August continues into September, no one is surprised. There is always a hint of smoke in the air, even as the fires are reported to be more and more contained to the north. Some nights I still can't sleep in the tree house, the smoke is so thick.

I itch to get outside, and so I wander the trails above the Yuba River or along its shore, away from the area that burned, as much as I can. I swim alone, thinking of Nicole, wondering if she will ever come to the river and find me here.

And if she does, will she be carrying a gun?

How will she react? How will I?

I try to imagine her as her most relaxed self—the girl who kissed me in the tree house—stripping down and jumping into the cold water to swim with me, but my brain always stops short, not wanting to really go there. Something is seriously wrong with me if I can't fantasize about a girl, but there is this sense of not wanting to torture myself with things I can't have. I fear if I allow myself to want Nicole, to really want her, nothing else will ever satisfy me.

I want to visit her, but I don't. I know, with her father back, it will only cause her trouble. I stay clear, and I hear gunshots in the distance, which always make me flinch. I know the gunfire comes from her property, since the sound came with her family's arrival and was rarely heard around here before then.

I stay in the water until I can't stand the cold a second longer, and then I drag myself onto the shore and stretch out on the warm river rocks, letting the sun bake me. Because I did decide to go back to school—no sense in bailing out on my senior year, I realized at the last second—I force myself to think about my final project, which is supposed to somehow be the culmination of all I've learned during my years of school. I am studying populations of local bees, and after spending the past two years planting bee-friendly plants around the area, and encouraging others to do so, I have to do final counts to see if my efforts have paid off, compile all my research, make sense of it, and consider all the factors that might make the numbers vary—of which there are many. Like the wildfires, for instance. Will they have made the bees go elsewhere?

The sound of gravel crunching underfoot catches my attention, and I sit up to see a sight my eyes have trouble believing is real.

Nicole is making her way down the hillside trail. She moves just as naturally, as unaware of her own grace, as she did the first time I saw her, and my stomach fills with a warm buzz. I don't know if she sees me here, since she's looking down at the trail to choose her steps carefully, but then when it levels out she looks up and straight at me.

## NICOLE

When I didn't find Wolf at the tree house, it was easy enough to guess where he might be on a day as hot as this. From above, shielded by the trees, I watch him swim, his bare chest glistening in the sun. I can remember all too well how his skin feels to touch, how his warmth and his scent are all I need to know when we're together.

I don't know what I'm waiting for. I came here to talk to him, but I don't know what I want to say.

Finally, when he is lying in the sun next to the river, I work up the nerve to go to him and see what kind of words come out.

I don't even know if he'll want to see me after I sent him away last month and after I blasted a hole in the wall to scare him away.

"Hey," I say when I'm close enough to be heard over the dull roar of the river.

"Hey yourself."

His hair wet and falling in thick strands around his face, he looks even more gorgeous than usual, and for a moment I can't think of a thing to say, so I sit down next to him and look out at the water.

"Come for a swim?"

"No, but now that I'm here it sounds like a good idea."

"You've been missed."

I look at him to see if he's joking, but he isn't. "My dad came back," I say.

"I know."

"It's been kind of awful."

"Are you okay?"

"Yeah," I say, and it's true. I am starting to be okay.

"What about your mom?"

"I guess she's gone for good. It's crazy, but I don't know. It makes sense in a weird way."

I tell him about my parents, their differences, my father's career-ending affair, my mother's decision to leave for good. Getting it all out in the open leaves me feeling like it's not so shameful. It's just life. Stuff happens, and you deal with it.

Wolf, next to me, silent, is the kind of person who listens with his whole self. He doesn't have to make the sort of I'm-listening sounds other people make, because there's never any doubt that his attention is on me.

This quality, as much as any other, makes me sure he is one of the rarest people I've ever met, like some exotic, endangered species.

"So is your dad okay with your mom being gone for good?"

I laugh. "He is the opposite of okay with it."

Neither of us says anything for a while. A hawk swoops overhead and lands on the branch of a nearby tree, and we watch as it rests for a bit and then sets off again, across the river.

"Listen," I say. "About what happened the day of the evacuation, I'm sorry."

"That's the first time I've ever been shot at."

"I wasn't shooting at you. I was shooting at the wall. To scare you away."

"Why?"

And then I tell him about what happened with Izzy and Kiva, how there was no way she could have gotten in a van and left with him.

He listens, his silence like a whole other person sitting next to us. Finally he says, "I wish you'd told me before. That fucking idiot—"

"Please, don't say anything. She just wants to move on, and I don't see what else there is to be done. Okay?"

He sits silent for a while, and then he nods.

"So anyway, my dad's been freaking out about Mom, but he decided to let us go to the school in town, and things have gotten kind of better since school started. He's just been working on the house, and we get to be gone all day."

"So what do you think of the school?"

"I think it would be better if you were there."

He gives me an odd look, like he doesn't know if I'm joking or serious.

"I guess our school wasn't an option for you?" he says.

I laugh. "Not in a million years. But it's okay. Izzy's always wanted to go to a regular high school, so it's her dream come true, and I'm just happy to be away from our house all day."

"Izzy's okay too?"

I give this some thought. I've never been close to Izzy, but lately things are better somehow. She talks to me. Asks me questions and advice. It's like, without our mom around, I'm the only person she has to rely on.

"She is. I mean, I can tell she's not as fearless as she used to be, but going to school has been a good thing for her. She loves getting away from Dad and being around normal kids all day."

I know he's thinking of what happened in the barn and how badly that might have shaken her, but he doesn't say anything else about it, and I'm glad. I'm done talking about it, agonizing over how I might have protected her, and explaining away all the things that went wrong.

I guess, in the end, it's another way we proved ourselves capable of surviving whatever circumstances were thrown at us. Without Dad's help.

"Feel like a swim?" Wolf asks, and I watch as he stretches and stands up.

"Sure," I say, conscious now that I didn't bring a swimsuit. He's wearing nothing but a pair of black boxer briefs.

I consider yet again what my father would say about this scenario, and I know, in a moment of true clarity, that it doesn't matter. It will never really matter to me again. He's not the one I have to answer to anymore. After all that's happened this summer, I answer to no one but myself. He can kick me out of the house if he wants to.

I'll still find a way to survive.

I stand up, too, and without thinking about it I take off my jeans, my top, leaving only my panties. I meet Wolf's gaze for a second and I don't know what I see in his eyes. Amusement, maybe?

I don't care.

I go to the water's edge and, without feeling for the temperature, without hesitating, I just keep walking until I'm knee deep, and then I jump the rest of the way in. The water is like an electric shock, taking my breath away with its absolute ice cold, with the stunning relief of it. I plunge beneath and then break the surface, gasping.

When I turn, Wolf is right behind me, already drenched, smiling and laughing.

"Just stay in it for a minute and you'll get used to the temperature," he says.

I go under again, and when I come back up for air he's a little closer, only an arm's reach away.

A wind has picked up in the past half hour, and the sky

above us, which has been a murky gray from the forest fires, is clearer now, a crystalline blue, for the first time in days.

I reach out and take Wolf's hand in mine. I don't know what I have in mind when I do this, but the moment we touch, I know. I pull him closer until he's up against me, our wet, cold bodies skin on skin. And I kiss him.

It is the best thing I've ever felt. I think of the way food tastes so much better when you've been really, truly hungry, and maybe that's how it is with us.

I have been really and truly hungry for this.

His arms slide around my waist and I am lost in the taste of his lips, the feel of his touch on my skin. I am wrapped up in the one and only person in the world I can completely trust.

I pull away a fraction of an inch to catch my breath and look into his watchful animal eyes.

"Are you still okay?" he asks.

"I'm more than okay."

The cold water has become a pleasant sensation now, numbing but welcome. I feel like there's so much I want to say, but no single statement comes to mind. I can only hope my silence speaks volumes.

"I've missed you," he says.

"Yeah?"

"Yeah."

"I've missed you too," I say. "I realized something, when I was trying to stay away."

"That you can't live without me?"

I smile at this.

"I realized how much I like being with you."

He kisses me again, this time slow and exploring. Somewhere overhead, a hawk calls. The sun blazing down on us warms our bare skin and we are, at that moment, the happiest creatures in this forest. We are a part of every living thing around us, and we are a whole world unto ourselves.